I0554534

One Week In Venice

A Tale of Quantum Mystery

PETER LUCIA

ISBN: 0-9741139-2-1
ISBN-13: 978-0-9741139-2-0

Cover design by Peter Lucia with Laura Basset

Peter Lucia Projects, Tinton Falls, NJ

DEDICATION

For Angela-DeVito Lucia—
With love and gratitude beyond space-time.

GLOSSARY OF ITALIAN AND VENETIAN WORDS

Calle: A typical Venetian street or lane, often narrow. It also refers to the streets of Venice in general. *Calle* replaces the word *via,* used elsewhere in Italy.

Campiello: A small campo. (See *Campo* below.)

Campo: A Venetian piazza or square. In Venice the word *piazza* is reserved almost exclusively for the Piazza San Marco. (Plural: campi)

Cortile: A small courtyard.

Fondamenta: A canal-side pedestrian walkway.

Nizioleto: A Venetian street sign.

Piazzetta: The "little piazza" along the west side of the Ducal Palace, connected to the Piazza San Marco.

Ponte: Bridge.

Rio: A small "regular" canal, the most numerous kind on the city. In Venice the word *canale* is usually reserved for the Grand Canal (Canal Grande) and a couple of other large waterways. In English *canal* is used for all Venetian water routes. (Plural: Rii)

Riva: A bank that runs alongside a large expanse of water such as the Bacino (the "basin" opposite the San Marco Area and the Riva degli Schiavoni).

Salizada: A paved street. While other streets in Venice are paved, historically *salizade* were the first to be paved. They retain this distinction in their name.

Scuola: A school or confraternity.

Sestiere: A district-division of Venice. Venice is divided into six *sestieri:* Cannaregio, Castello, Dorsoduro, San Marco, and Santa Croce.

Sotopòrtego: A squared-off tunnel-like passage that cuts through a building or buildings and leads from one area to another, such as from a campo to a corte, from a fondamenta to a salizada and so forth. A sotopòrtego that runs alongside a canal is usually open at the canal side.

Vaporetto: A Venetian water bus, the most common form of public transportation in and around Venice.

Je connais un pays étrange
où les lions volent et marchent les pigeons.

— Jean Cocteau

Chapter One

They are an apparition as much as an appearance: the Venetian carnival queens. Their ballooned-out gowns of bejeweled and beaded satin, stiffly inflated and richly colored, cascade below turbans heaped with every sort of fluff. They are floats unto themselves, these ladies. As they inch across the Piazzetta or posture near parked gondolas on the Riva degli Schiavoni, their full-face masks are frozen with indifference, disengaged from the hordes of modern tourists around them.

But one of them, one night, screamed.

She stumbled against the harsh bricks of the narrow *calle*, steadied her turban. The eye-holes twitched in her tranquil cover as she stared at the large dark heap of sluggish muscle writhing seven or eight meters above her. *What...what is it?* The huge thing was atop the old neighborhood arch. *It's...an animal!* The beast roared at the sky, fangs glinting in the moonlight of the Santa Croce neighborhood.

Her mask half off, Ornella cried out; she looked to the corner a short distance away and tried to call her big sister, who paused to chat on her way home from the ball, but her voice was a mute white flash in her mind. She scurried under the arch and into her home three doors away. Trembling all over, she told her brother-in-law to call the police. He refused. Was she high or crazy or both? She dialed 1-1-3 herself and then collapsed.

The police saw nothing. Her relatives saw nothing. The beast on the arch had vanished.

***

Several hours earlier on the night of Ornella Ruisi's scream, Tonio Occhini, a student from Milan, was hoping against hope that he would not throw up in public. It was his huge fluorescent-green backpack that hunched him over, but the better (or worst) part of his crippled gait and half-asleep demeanor came from too much partying. *"Oddio"* (Oh God), he groaned.

Leaving Piazza San Marco and its ever-growing crowd, he staggered out of the dark connecting arcade and into the lightning-white shock of studio lights. He grimaced, shielded his eyes. The painful electric glare came from the equipment of a foreign TV crew parked at the basin-end of the Orseolo Canal. A show-and-tell was in progress on this the last night of *carnevale*. A few people in the basic costumes—Arlecchino, Colombina, Medico della Peste—were the objects of spirited analysis on the part of two carefully coiffed hosts. Tonio saw only a bright iridescent smear. Music thundering from the great piazza and into his brain further blurred the spectacle; and the emerald glow of the gondola-strewn canal made him feel he was in a dream.

All he cared about was to find a secluded corner before the sour turbulence in his stomach produced its own show. With hundreds of tourists crowding the *fondamenta*, and each with a camera, he felt sure he would find himself heaving on YouTube, from all angles, forever and ever. *"Oddio."* Huffing to keep down his sarde in saor (a sardine specialty he pigged on an hour before), he moved away from the mob, whose tall flame-like shadows writhed tauntingly on the building facades.

At last he was at the darker, less peopled end of the canal, at the foot of the diminutive Piavola Bridge. Dragging his backpack, he quickened his pace. The knowledge of a secluded *campo* on the other side encouraged him. Then, at the top of the bridge, as though invisible fingertips had touched his chest, he halted, wide-eyed. At first he thought it an odd reflection from the water, but the sight grew solid: Behind a grated window in a closed office building a baby floated in mid-air. The baby rippled, rippled red. *The baby is on fire!* Tonio gave a whimpering groan as the flames burned the tiny screaming face into a grimacing skull. He wobbled, reeled. To keep from falling forward he dashed full-tilt down the steps. He stumbled near the bottom and a white-capped patrolman seized his arm. *"Cosa combini, tu?"* (What are you up to?) The young man pointed frantically at the window—now vacant—above him. The policeman looked up. Tonio looked down. *"Cazzo!"* cried the officer as the puke sprayed his boots.

***

Rich Travella appreciated the carnival tradition but did not care to participate in its events. It was more like him — and unlike most other twenty-six-year-olds — to enjoy the knowledge that spirited life unfolded where he wasn't rather than where he was. He savored in itself his awareness of the grand balls that bloomed here and there in the salons of the city's fine hotels and weathered palaces — the otherworldly raiment, the glistering chandeliers, the familiar rise-and-fall of Vivaldi's smoothest strings (while avoiding thoughts of the carnival's raucous aspects). His away-from-the-action custom matched a pattern he noticed in his poetry: the depiction of a shaded zone, under an awning or in the shadow of a building, which looked on a sunny place a short distance beyond. He could step out of the shade if he wished to and walk to the other world; but he was not inclined to do so, only because he thrived on the thrilling possibilities with which his imagination infused it.

Except that this evening he really would be stepping out (after all, he was far from being a hermit). In the dusky blue light of his northwest gothic windows, he closed the cover on his laptop and leaned forward, elbows on the thick ebony dining table. He pushed up his glasses as if to see his thoughts more clearly. He considered himself fortunate that a few remarkable people, who truly enjoyed his company, accepted him into their circle. He was always surprised by his own surprise at how much people liked him; it was as if his unconscious had been telling him not to believe it. Nevertheless, he knew that tonight — the last night of *Carnevale*, Tuesday before the start of Lent — he would be a welcome guest at an extraordinary private party, one that even his "wallflower" imagination could not live up to.

Even so, he had to shake off the pang of pending society. With a breathy grunt he sprang from his chair and walked down the three wide steps to the living room of his sublet apartment. He knew how it was, though: He would end up having a great time and even be entertaining. It always happened. He found it curious that he needed to relearn this lesson each time he found an invitation in his hands.

He slapped a quick waltz on his thighs: *one*-two-three. "Just go and have fun!" he ordered himself in his native language, echoing the words of his mother back in Rhode Island. He immediately translated, *"Vacci e divertiti!"* It was an old oral exercise of his: whenever he spoke to himself aloud in English he would translate what he said into Italian.

Now he advised himself (silently) that it might be time to turn on a few lights. He snickered. His extreme love of pure window radiance was an aesthetic necessity — a lure for inspiration's glimmers — a habit he coddled to the point of practical inconvenience. Like right now. He switched on a couple of girandola lamps and made for the bathroom to shave.

His face was narrower than it was round. He possessed a thick head of dark brown hair and wore tortoise-shell horn-rimmed glasses. These were the scholarly "owl-eye" type, which he kept on while shaving. Though a scholar in fact, he thought he resembled the silent film comic Harold Lloyd. He looked a little less pale, however, and a lot more serious than the actor (a gravity undone by the occasional wall-collision when lost in thought). A great fan of old movies and anything antique, he was pleased with his "retro" appearance.

He dried his face and went to the bedroom to take out his rented tuxedo. Seconds after he switched on the ceiling light, he noted a quavering glow outside one of the three casement windows. He adjusted his glasses and moved toward the curiosity; then he spun around and switched off the light. He saw a fidgety blotch of yellow fire on the far side of the terracotta rooftops. It was the flame of a torch. There was movement too, human movement. He saw a hand holding the torch, then the sunken eyes of a flickering face. A withered old man in an antique doublet and tricorn hat squatted in a corner of the opposite roof. His disarranged clothing and contorted posture gave Rich the impression he had fallen from the sky. In the other hand he held on his chest a chunky object resembling a book.

Rich had never seen anyone out there before; he thought the adjacent lower rooftops inaccessible. He unlatched the window, opened it, leaned out. The chilly air did not smell burnt, as he thought it would, from the fire. "Are you all right down there?" he called out. "What are you doing?" The man emitted the long, panicked squeal of an axed pig. Rich felt spiders creep up the back of his neck. "Oh brother," he groaned in English, not bothering to translate. He scratched a lightning-fast sign of the cross on his chest and leaned out again. "Are you all right? Do you need help?" He felt a moral imperative using him as a ventriloquist's dummy. "If you need help, I'll get it! If this is a carnival prank...!" Then he grumbled in English, "A funny hat."

"I am the Leonardo!" the man cried wildly.

The guy's probably insane.

"Leonardo Tron! Possibility is mine!" He raised his book-like object.

"Careful with the fire!" He waved a wide *no-no* and then narrowed his eyes. He thought he saw streaks of blood on the old man's face behind the agitated flame. "All right, I'm going to call the police." He waited a moment to see if he reacted.

Damn, now I gotta deal with this.

He went for his cell phone, which he had left on the table. "A goddamn torch... He's got a goddamn torch and a funny hat." An officer answered the phone and Rich described the problem, quick to append a disclaimer about the unreality of the situation. As he spoke he returned to the bedroom and switched on the light so the mysterious man could see him on the phone. "Yes, sir, that's correct, Corte Tron. It's a small courtyard off Campo San Benedetto—San Beneto, I mean—beside the San Beneto church, in the *sestiere* of San Marco. Yes, across from the Fortuny Museum."

Even before hanging up he suspected the flame had expired or moved out of sight. He switched off the ceiling lamp and looked. "What the hell?" He stuck out his head and searched all around in the sapphire dusk—*"Where the hell?"*—as the six o'clock bell of a nearby church called from another world.

***

Rich felt it was summer, but a freakishly chilly one, as he strode past congregations of late-winter wanderers and revelers who had seized the city's crusty corridors the way they did in July. It was freakish also because of the costumes he saw: simple half-masks here, a couple of leopard-women there;

walking, blinking tarot cards; a three-headed jester with jangling bells on the crimson tusks of each silly cap.

The evening felt oddly troubled, too, not only because of a trend he perceived in bloody zombie costumes, but because of the appearance—and disappearance—of the weird old man on the roof.

Strange, very strange, how familiar…

It was one of those mental states in which aspects of a consuming event are not apparent until later.

I've seen that old man somewhere else.

He experienced this memory-phenomenon before and considered it a mild form of shock or a trick of adrenaline. He recalled his edginess at a lecture he gave at the University of Venice; the people he met after his talk, when he regained his calm, looked uncannily familiar as if they were ghosts from deep in his past.

"Comunque," he said in Italian, meaning *anyway*.

It was mild for the end of February and he perspired under his woolen coat. He was a swift, tireless walker and carried his dress shoes in a small briefcase under his arm. To avoid Piazza San Marco, the loud music, and the squeeze of people awaiting the fireworks, he chose a longer, wider course on his way to the party. The affair was at a well-concealed private palazzo a short stroll east of Saint Mark's. Leo "Nico" Leoni owned and presided over the grand centuries-old palace. He was a seventy-something bachelor of great wealth and legendary influence in international affairs. Having retired, he took to collecting people—people he liked—and enjoying himself. Simonetta Ballarin, his niece and owner of a free "around town" newspaper, had introduced him to Rich at a lecture months earlier. He met the man one other time, by chance, in front of

Antico Martini, an exclusive restaurant next to La Fenice, the historic theater. All smiles and animation, he invited Rich to dine with him. He phoned Simonetta and the three shared an unforgettable dinner, a bottle of fine wine apiece.

"Simonetta," he whispered as he entered spacious Campo Santa Maria Formosa. Her presence in his mind teased him with a flutter of affection. For one thing, he liked the way she pronounced his name: *Reech*. He blinked away the sentiments; but he laughed aloud (inciting the glance of a passerby), because *Santa Maria Formosa* meant *shapely Saint Mary*, and Simonetta was not at all shapely or voluptuous. She was more like an eel and about seven or eight centimeters taller than he was. Nor, he gathered, was she much of a saint; with a touch of regret her uncle had confided in him about the company she was keeping.

He passed the Formosa campanile and the great white church with its unruffled symmetries, enjoying the aroma of sauce and seafood as outdoor tables received their first diners. As in many other spots, Middle Eastern men flung toy parachutes high into the air, hoping potential purchasers would fancy their slow, blue-lighted descent. After another ten minutes of narrow lanes and unfamiliar bridges, one of which he crossed twice, he became aware of a stately drumbeat. He sensed it was following him. He forgot all about it when found himself close to where he thought he should be. Happily he saw people in formal attire; they looked confident in their destination. He backed into a doorway to change shoes and then trailed them. He made two or three tight turns by the rusty fortifications of windows and doors and then trod into a private *cortile*. Its lantern-topped columns and dolled-up arrivals emitted an aura of special circumstance.

The honeyed glow of lamplight and the mannered measures of a Boccherini quartet escaped from beyond an open arched doorway. Looking in, he saw that a marble "chessboard" floor led from the anteroom to a gilded desk flanked by men dressed in the style of the Vatican Swiss Guard. He could just make out the angular bowing movements of the string quartet behind them.

He sharpened his demeanor. He established a stern, no-nonsense face for the hallway attendants. He pushed back his shoulders and marched in—stumbling awkwardly. He shot an accusatory squint at the lip of stone beneath the doorway and tugged at his bow tie (he thought it might start twirling, an effect altogether out of spirit with the music).

At the desk two "Swiss Guards" took his coat and case; they examined his fancy invitation; this was framed inside a pocket-sized wallet of black and turquoise satin and embossed with the winged lion of Saint Mark, the ubiquitous symbol of Venice. The lion's paw-touched book was so clearly rendered he easily made out its famous words: *Pax tibi Marce, evangelista meus. Hic requiescet corpus tuum.* (Peace be unto you, Mark, my evangelist. Here your body will rest.) People in classic carnival dress drifted about decoratively. The space was once part of a larger floor later divided into a reception. Aside from the panels of laguna-green marble, all the classical moldings—soaring pilasters and arches encrusted with swags, pendants, and sea creatures—were clearly original to the building. More recent were the trompe d'oeil wall-renderings of Renaissance dandies, who from behind faux-painted windows and balustrades gazed down with mute assessment on the arriving guests. The idea was right out of Palladio's Villa Barbaro, and it made him feel that he was the invading fiction in the midst of their reality.

At the point of ascending the ceremonial staircase, he again became aware of the drumbeat he had noted earlier. He drew back from the stairs. Into in the hall marched the drummer himself, all done up with embroidered doublet, jerkin, striped trunk-hose breeches and floppy muffin cap. A line of highly coiffed, nubile girls followed — a radiant dozen of them; they wore brown floor-length tunics trimmed with sparkling gold and carried wicker baskets, whose contents of rosebuds they joyfully scattered.

"La Festa delle Marie," someone announced, referring to the Festival of the Maries, the elaborate beauty-queen event that opened the carnival ten days earlier. With half-serious majesty, a young man at the desk called out, "A personal variation courtesy of Signor Leo 'Nico' Leoni!"

As Rich waited for the parade to make its way up the stairs, he felt someone move in close behind him. He did not look back; he assumed it was a person he knew trying to be playful, most likely Simonetta. But now the cushiony bosom pressing into his back ruled against it being her. The strong, hot, yellow-red perfume was not right either. Hands slowly smoothed his sides, slid something into his pocket; he felt a mouth come closer and closer as if to kiss his ear.

The warm lips whispered, "Tron."

He made a move to turn around but the woman held his shoulders as if to enforce a "no-looking" rule. A moment later he disobeyed; he glimpsed a lady in a patchwork Colombina costume and curly brown wig slip through an arched doorway. He heaved a puzzled sigh and started up the stairs. He wondered why she said "Tron." Corte Tron was the courtyard he lived on. Another coincidence struck him: The old man on the roof called himself Tron, Leonardo Tron. He had almost forgotten. *Tron* was an old Venetian family name (from *Trono* or *Truno*). There was a Doge Tron, he recalled, Niccolò, fifteenth century. A number of sites in Venice bore this historical patrician name.

Under the laughing eyes and pointing finger of a frescoed Renaissance boy, Rich moved to one side atop the staircase to let others pass. He fished in his pocket for whatever it was the woman put there. He drew out a stiff circular disk of paper with another, smaller disk flush on top of it. A black bead joined the two in the center. The bead acted as a hub allowing the smaller disk to be turned like a dial. The Greek alphabet, in capitals, banded the edge of both pieces. He knew what it was—a cipher disc, a simple instrument for decoding messages by way of letter substitution. Back in its day, the Venetian Republic employed highly complex ones for the communication of top-secret intelligence. He wondered whether the present specimen was a party favor to be used in a game or raffle. Leo, he understood, loved to involve people in practical jokes and playful scenarios. He gazed down the stairs at the other arriving guests. No one whispered in their ears or handed them anything.

Comunque...

He slid the device into his pocket and prepared his entrance, starting with a speedy sign of the cross. He knew he would have to switch from "dashing captain of industry" to "maladjusted loner," his default approach; he was not sure why, but he sensed that a touch of gawky shyness would make things easier, paradoxically absorb his genuine feeling of awkwardness. He pursed his lips and moved them to one side. He raised an eyebrow and pushed up one shoulder, fixing it in place. Boccherini's strings gave way to Cole Porter's keys as he scuffed into the long *primo piano nobile* (principal living level) with its polished floors and foreshortened line of Murano chandeliers.

Leo 'Nico' Leoni came at him with open arms and welcoming roar. *"Caro amico!"* The sturdy gray-bearded man embraced him; he looked him in the eyes at arm's length and gave him a hearty shake. "Thank you for coming!" Rich had the impression that a vodka-filled Cossack (in a red bow tie) had just greeted him. "But what did you do to yourself? You look like *il gobbo.*"

"*Il gobbo...gobbo?*" He drew a blank on the word.

"You know, *il gobbo di Notre-Dame.*"

Rich straightened himself up. "Oh no, I'm okay, thank you. Thank you for inviting me, signore."

"As opposed to *il Gobbo di Rialto*; you know that statue? But he's not really a *gobbo*; he's just overworked. Oh, excuse me." Leo switched to English and seized the arm of a man standing near him. "Ambassador, let me introduce my good friend Doctor Richard Travella, formerly of Princeton University. Rich Travella, this is His Excellency, Ambassador..." Rich did not catch the name or the country of the thin, swarthy diplomat (the use of *doctor* in front of his name always threw him off). Leo laughed and grasped their shoulders, forcing a huddle. "I have to tell you, Aazaad," he confided, "I was at a lecture recently which Doctor Travella gave at the university here." He laughed again, nearly buckling over. "After he finished, there was a discussion in English and someone tossed out that famous old saying of George Santayana, 'Those who cannot remember the past are doomed to repeat it.' I agree with the sentiment, absolutely, but I have to tell you I'm tired of hearing people say it again and again and again. So, without even a blink, Doctor Travella comes out with, 'Yes, and those who know Santayana's adage are doomed to repeat *it* also.' I nearly fell off my chair! I used to say the same thing; I thought I owned the joke. I had to meet this fellow!"

Leo's story was a minor revelation to him. He had assumed it was his lecture — *Eliade's Concept of Hierophany from the Dolce Stil Novo to Montale* — that stirred him. "Well," he fretted, "I felt a little bad afterward. I didn't want to embarrass the guy."

"What embarrass? He laughed his ass off! You know, it's even more annoying in Italian. We make it rhyme: *'Chi non coltiva la memoria è condannato a ripetere la storia.'*"

Rich wondered if the poor ambassador, who stood there nodding with a beamingly genial smile, had understood a single word of the whole conversation.

"Okay, Rich, look, go have a good time, eat, drink. It's *Martedì Grasso*, remember, *Mardi Gras*, so enjoy yourself. Go find your girlfriend. She's bored, she told me. Imagine that, a niece of mine, bored!"

Rich felt his face heat up, saw it redden in his mind. He wondered if Leo thought she was actually his girlfriend.

"Go rescue her from any riffraff she may have dragged in."

Is she really my girlfriend?

He and Simonetta had encountered each another at a couple of events. They had lunch together only once. He often ran into her on the street but never saw her with the "riffraff" Leo mentioned. In fact, he had never seen her with anyone except Leo. They emailed back and forth a half a dozen times; she raved about Rich's photographs and poems, which he included as attachments.

"And stop calling me *signore*. He's so formal with me. Use *tu* with your old friend. Italy is a democracy."

Rich cleared his throat. "A democracy, yes, I can see that," and he swept an open hand to indicate the fabulous room and the dozens of expensively attired guests, as well as the "Maries," who now floated silver trays of spectacular food.

Leo laughed in a low staccato moan. "See what I mean? He comes right out with them, on cue!"

Rich winced an apology and took his leave.

He never thought himself a disarming wit. It was that certain traits emerged with certain people. Leo was incredibly *simpatico*; Italian and English verbiage flowed easily in his company. He came off as family, even if Rich had never had a family member with a background like his; he heard it involved the manipulation of international players on a grand scale; that he had been an independent contractor, a *condottiere diplomatico* or diplomatic soldier-of-fortune. He chuckled. The shaking that Leo gave him at the door had certainly manipulated *him*, lessened his edginess. Even so, he took a glass of champagne and suspected he would need eight or ten more before he socially relaxed.

In one gulp the flounder-faced, wiry-haired piano player downed most of his red wine and dug into *Anything Goes*. Rich threaded his way among the guests, weaving as discreetly as possible with finely calibrated cordiality. No cozy corners behind the groupings of period tables and chairs, no shadowed hiding places, presented themselves. On the contrary, the many gilt-framed mirrors about the room multiplied his exposure.

Wait a second.

Rich pushed up his eyeglasses. Reflected in the mirrors was a familiar-looking man, a doubly familiar-looking man. Or was he triply familiar? He looked a lot like the raggedy old fellow on the roof he saw earlier: short gray beard, boney face. He was the opposite of untidy now: Hair combed into a curly gray wave, he wore a tailored tuxedo and shiny patent leather shoes. He held a drink and conversed with a meticulously assembled woman in a red and silver gown, a supermodel type.

Now he saw in the mirror one of Leo's assistants, a middle-aged hipster with tinted Ferrari glasses. His name was Gigio Mattone; they had met before. The broad-shouldered character was approaching him from behind. He sharpened himself for social contact and about-faced, holding out his hand. *"Buona sera.* How are you?"

"You still at the university?" Gigio asked evenly.

"Well, no, that was a temporary appointment." He shrugged his shoulders and rocked his head. "Now I'm just...hanging around, studying, writing, photograph-ing reflections in the canals, textures." He thought of adding, 'till I run out of money' but did not want to give hints as crafty freeloaders do when they are looking for a handout.

"Creative stuff," Gigio put in. "Sounds like you're walking in the footsteps of John Ruskin."

Rich's mouth fell open. He had not expected this "bouncer" to come out with the name of the great nineteenth-century art critic who had spent half a lifetime scrupulously studying Venice's artistic and architectural heritage.

Rich laughed. "Ruskin? Well, I wouldn't go that far."

After more personal patter, he tightened his brow and asked Gigio if he knew the man over there who looked so familiar to him.

"Oscar Fantini," Gigio told him. "He's an actor. You've probably seen him in a movie or a play. Would you like to meet him?" Rich politely declined. He was at the point of relating the strange story of the man's lookalike when one of Leo's wandering assistants called Gigio aside.

The piano player downed another full glass of wine and started in with *Begin the Beguine.* Rich meandered to the end of the room, near the crowded ebony bar. He noticed an alluring arch and what he suspected was a parallel series of rooms. He zeroed in on it. Right then he heard his Smartphone play a cycle of robotic-sounding *whoops* he identified as his Skype account. He took out the phone and slipped behind a potted palm.

It was Simonetta. Her small pert face, framed by her jet black dutch-boy hair, smiled on the diminutive screen. As ever, she reminded Rich of the silent-movie stars Colleen Moore or Louise Brooks. He imagined that the bias toward one or the other shifted in accordance with her attitude, be it good-girl or bad-girl. He was unsure which polarity she assumed at present.

"Where are you, *tesorino?*" (little treasure) she asked, pushing her face right up to the pinhole lens of her phone.

"I'm here, keeping company with a...*Chrysalidocarpus lutescens*, the tag says, but don't quote me. Where are *you?*"

"Go to the bar. Find Franco the bartender. He's the blond guy with the ring in his ear and bad teeth. Looks like a pirate."

Rich did as she asked; he held up his phone for Franco between the heads of people at the bar, wondering whether this "pirate" was one of the "riffraff" her uncle referred to. "Ciao, Simonetta!" Franco rasped loudly. Other people shoved their faces in front of the phone to greet her and ask where she was. Rich felt no grief in the center of the action. He bounced on his toes, happy that Simonetta's virtual presence had cushioned his actual presence. He felt special for her having singled him out.

Maybe she really is my girlfriend.

She told Franco to give Rich a bottle of extra-cold (*freddo freddo*) champagne and two glasses.

"*Beato lui!*" (Lucky him!) Franco declared.

With two glasses and the cold-cold Moët clawed in one hand, Simonetta's talking face in the other, he followed her directions. He left the crowded salon, passed through a series of sitting rooms and then wide-eyed entered a magnificent two-story library whose mahogany shelves hosted thousands of books.

"It's a little out of the way, but I thought you'd like to see the old family library. Leo's quite proud of it."

"*Stupenda!* I could live in here. Stained glass windows!"

She guided him across two rooms in the opposite direction; then she sent him down a spiral stairway; he felt he was in a giant iron corkscrew as he half-consciously counted the steps and twistingly descended to the original part of the entrance hall. This section of the floor was a chilly, lamp-lighted court with a decorative wellhead, chubby shrubs in urns, and a colonnaded pathway around the perimeter. Behind him he noted the arched door that opened to the reception area.

"Tesorinooo!"

He saw Simonetta only from the shoulders up, and indistinctly at that; she was just beyond the double doorway leading to the side canal. Clearly she was sitting in a boat.

"What is *that!*" Rich exclaimed as he neared her.

"My *gondoletta.* It's electric. All fiberglass body." She rapped her knuckles on it. "Hop in!"

It was less than half the length of a regular gondola, a little higher at the sides and plumper, a cartoon caricature of the real thing. Two red vinyl seats, each wide enough to tightly accommodate three people, faced each other.

"Uncle Leo called me and said you were here. No, sit here, close to me, I've got a blanket."

"He called you?"

"Wow, I've never seen you without a button-down collar. You look good. Go ahead, sit." She grasped the steering stick and turned a knob on the front console. The boat slowly and almost soundlessly but for the slight water-wash moved forward, its chrome beak appearing to cleave the black-green paisley water, the moon and window reflections rolling, rippling, glimmering.

"They let you ride this around town?"

"Sure, it's a private boat. It's got a navigation-light. I stick to the quieter *rii*, though. I have it for a week. The gondoliers love it. They think I'm eccentric."

Rich popped the champagne cork. "You, eccentric?"

He loved sitting low in the canals, deep between the close, sheltering walls of palaces. On land, he noted, one's smallness is less profound even before much larger edifices. He felt he was in the body of Venice, a corpuscle in its bloodstream; that no matter how wonderful the walking-part of the city was, no matter how familiar one was with its lanes, the water-part was the other half of the story, the true revelation of its amphibious nature.

"M'mmm...I love champagne when the weather's chilly. Come on, get under the blanket. Put your head back, watch the sky and the housetops move by. It's neat when the bridges come over."

"Just keep your eye on the road." He nodded at her glass. "Isn't this considered drunk driving?"

"Sure, but I know all the cops around here. Relax." She slid her slim fingers over the top of his and rubbed them.

He adjusted his position and moved his hand away. "An odd thing happened tonight, a couple of hours before I left the house." He narrated his experience with the old man on the roof, detailing it as engagingly as one would a ghost story. In the middle of the tale, Simonetta parked her craft just beyond the Calle Furlani Bridge, near the handsome white façade of the Scuola di San Giorgio degli Schiavoni. She sat holding the blanket up to her chin same as a frightened child, algae-green eyes wide.

"Well, the police came and I was a little embarrassed. Me there in my tuxedo. They had this look on their faces. Let's say it was verging on skeptical. Carnival night and all that. They searched outside the window with their flashlights."

Simonetta lowered her blanket and gently bounced, as if bouncing generated thoughts.

"Didn't anyone else, neighbors, see him up there?"

"Well, this has been haunting me a bit too, besides the guy looking familiar. That spot up there is isolated. It's recessed a little, down. I *think* I'm the only person who can see the roof, or rooftops. My apartment is higher than the others on that end of the courtyard. So I have the peculiar feeling—it's hard to describe—the feeling that this bizarre show was put on just for me."

"That's really *strange*, Reech!" She shot one of her ear-splitting, one-note laughs but settled down quickly with a thoughtful hum. Then she pointed at him. "You know, I had a creepy encounter tonight, too. Weird." She downed the rest of her glass and handed it to Rich. "I was on my way here, *in gondoletta.* What happened is I pulled over for a moment because I couldn't find my phone. There was this kid, a teenager, who saw me. He looked really sick, a total mess; I mean like sick from getting too much into...whatever he was into. Tonio was his name. He was lost. He asked if I knew where a certain campo was; he was staying with friends over in Cannareggio. So I took him part of the way, and he tells me this story about how he was walking over the Piavola Bridge—that's the bridge over the Rio Orseolo, you know, by the Banca Nazionale del Lavoro there; he was walking over the bridge and he said he saw...he saw a *flaming baby,* he said, in a window on the other side, a floating flaming baby. Ha! So I'm thinking, *Accidenti!* I picked up another *squilibrato!* Why do I attract weirdos!" She started laughing; it was one of her long, self-absorbed chortles, as if she were laughing at her own laughing, a trait Rich found cute. She settled down and wiped her eyes. "Oh God, I'm overrevving." She let out another hiccup-like ear-drum-splitter. "Sorry!" She rounded

PETER LUCIA

her lips and blew. "Anyway, it was a strange story, and it ended with him throwing up on a cop. Ha!"

Rich was squinting, itching his lip. He held up a finger. "Listen—" She grasped his finger and pulled it toward her mouth. "No, don't bite me, Simonetta." She let go and looked down, snickering and gently bobbing. Now he started in. "L-L-Listen..." Laughter overtook him. Simonetta shot another ear-splitter. "You are so funny," he gushed. He inhaled deeply, exhaled. "Look, that bridge the kid was on, the Piavola. I know that bridge... No, wait a second." He pulled from his pocket the cipher disk. "Did you get one of these? Somebody slipped it into my pocket when I came in."

She took the disk and closely examined it in the moonlight. "No, I didn't. What is it, a decoder-thing?

"Yes, a cipher disk. It's used for—"

"I got *this*, though." She took from her shiny black purse a folded piece of paper and handed it to him. "A guy dressed as Arlecchino gave it to me and mumbled something in my ear."

"Yes! What did he say?"

"Sounded like *trong.*"

"No, it was *Tron,* the old Venetian surname. The Colombina who gave me the disk said the same thing to me—*Tron.* I'm sure of it. This is really... The guy on the roof called himself Tron, I told you. But there's... Wait, let me look it this." He removed his glasses and squinted closely at the stiff, colorless page. Typed words, complete Greek ones, embellished it. Like the cipher disk, it had the rough feel of old parchment. "Did anyone else get stuff like this, do you know?"

"I showed the message to a few people, Uncle Leo too. He *said* he'd never seen it before, but... Can you read it?"

"Looks like nonsense words at this point. My guess is that my disk is supposed to be used to decode your message."

"H'mmm." Her almond eyes wandered. "A certain somebody's up to something."

"Leo. I get that much."

"He's always been a trickster, Reech."

"I'm aware of that, but—"

"You don't know the half of it, a *tenth* of it. But I'm sure this has to do with the party."

"But it's the *Tron* thing... Listen... What I was going to say was, the bridge, the one the kid was on when he supposedly saw the baby on fire or whatever it was you said."

"Yes, the Piavola Bridge."

"*Piavola* means *doll* in Venetian, no?"

"Right, it's a dainty little bridge. It's famous. So you think he knew the name and imagined a baby doll or something?"

"No, that's not it, but you've got a point there. The thing is, the weird thing—it's another coincidence I guess—the thing is that the bridge has another name, doesn't it?"

Simonetta thought for a moment. "Oh Oh Oh! *Tron.* Yes! That's its first name actually—Ponte Tron o De La Piavola. Tron's the name of the calle also, which leads to it."

"Now, Simonetta, where do I live? The courtyard my building is on? It's Corte Tron!"

She stared fixedly at Rich as she pondered these parallels.

"So it's two weird things tonight both in a Tron location, you might say. Then there's a 'Leonardo Tron' on the roof. Then two people whisper *Tron* to us and give us the note and the disk."

They stayed wordless for a moment.

Rich broke the silence with a chuckle. "I saw somebody at the party who looked a lot like the old guy on the roof. Gigio told me he was an actor."

"It must have been Oscar Fantini." She rubbed her chin. "This sounds like a big one." I think maybe... I wonder..."

"You think maybe..."

"Yes. But I don't know. Guy on your roof in a costume. It does have that feeling, but a *big* feeling, I mean, which is like—"

"Do you really...?"

"Uncle Leo."

"You think?" He made a strained face. "Is he really so...elaborate with his pranks? No, it can't be. How could it?"

"Let's go inside, tesorino, get something to eat."

The party had become more crowded and noisy than before and Rich doubled up on his social grin, knowing that his jaw would ache in the morning. He nodded at the piano player whose bow tie, he noted, was now coming undone; the fellow inhaled more wine and was torn between Gershwin's *Just One of Those Things* and Porter's *I get a Kick Out of You.*

They found Leo with a small crowd around him. With much animation, he explained to an English lady the proper use of the word *sprezzatura*, which she had used incorrectly; she had intended it to stand in for the English slang word *cool* or *suave*. "You see, sometimes in Italian you can put an *s* in front of a word to turn it into its opposite. You have *contento*, or *happy*; you put an *s* in front and it becomes *sconteno* or *unhappy*, *discontented*. The word *sprezzatura* contains *prezzo*, the Italian word for *price;* in fact *apprezzare* means *to place value* on a thing. By putting an *s* in front of it you're negating the price, so to speak. That is, you make whatever you do or say look *so natural and easy*, even unimportant to you, that no one would ever guess the price you must have paid to be—or to appear—so accomplished. That's sprezzatura. No one would ever guess you prepared your performance or your knowledge in advance, perhaps with great effort. In my opinion, you should never tell a person he has good sprezzatura, because then you would be telling him that he is less than a god." He and everyone around him laughed. "My good friend Richard Travella here, Doctor Travella, I'm sure can tell you the historical use of the word."

Rich widened his eyes and swallowed his champagne with an audible gulp. He heard Simonetta stifle a laugh. "Well, it's usually called 'the art of artlessness.'" He started in with a jittery two-step but stopped when Simonetta smacked his elbow. "It comes out of the Renaissance, notably in Castiglione's *Il libro del cortegiano*, which is a book about how to make a big splash at court, though we find similar expressions before that, in Boccaccio's *Decameron*, for example. Of course, there's the ancient, Latin saying *'ars est celare artem'*—'art is to conceal art'—or Ovid's *'Si latet ars, prodest'*—'if art is hidden it is useful.' In the final analysis, it's a highly developed act of deception."

Now he saw a made-to-order opening to rib Leo again, on the basis of his reputation as a prankster. "The concept of *ingannare*, which in Italian means *to deceive"*—he leaned toward Leo and all but touched him with spread-out fingertips—"is a recurring thing in Italian literature, either as out-and-out deception or as philosophy or as a fascinating play between the mask and the face, so to speak, illusion and reality. It's all over the place. It runs from Boccaccio and the *novellino* form of that period through Ariosto to, of course, Pirandello, Bufallino..."

Throughout Rich's discourse, Leo stood still with a tight-lipped, stoic look of a person who struggles to restrain a comment. "Bravo!" he cried at last. "His account makes me nostalgic for my late profession, which, I might add, helped to bring about elections where machetes instead of ballots would have ruled the day. But you forgot to add Machiavelli!"

Indeed, and the Venetian, Goldoni. What about Shakespeare's Portia? *Two Gentlemen from Verona...?* Hey, wherever you find Italians..." This provoked an array of cackles. He toasted Leo and finished off his champagne. "Of course, ingenious artifice can arise from necessity." He said this in deference to Leo's late profession, which he knew involved political persuasion and probably a lot of *ingannare.* "You'll have to tell us of your excellent adventures, Leo."

"Sure, come back in fifty years."

As not to appear in collusion, Simonetta had withdrawn at the start of Rich's comments about deception. Wearing a well-pressed smirk, she stood in front of a sideboard, decorating a plate with moist Venetian *cicchetti.*

"I need more champagne," Rich said secretively. "I do believe I'm starting to lose touch with reality."

"Well then, maybe you'll appreciate the Dalí exhibit at the Diocesano. We can go there tomorrow."

"That's all I need."

She handed him an artist's palette of stuffed artichoke bottoms, truffle ravioli, a pile of risotto di go', baccalà mantecato, grilled razor clams, and a tiny octopus, which Rich named Ottino and said he would not eat but take home as a pet.

"So I'm thinking," he continued, "let's see where it leads. Let's not say anything. If nothing comes of it here, I'll try my hand at the message when I get home. I'm good at puzzles. I'll bet it's only the disk and the message, though." He made a sour face and shook his head. "The other stuff is just coincidence." Nevertheless, he scanned the room for Oscar Fantini, the actor who resembled the old man on the roof.

"I don't know, Reech."

"It's probably a fun thing. Maybe there's a door prize involved."

Simonetta murmured, "Only for us?"

Rich shrugged.

The piano player finished a quirky, syncopated rendition of *Smoke Gets in Your Eyes*. With a crooked grin he broke into *Funiculì, Funiculà*, a spirited Neapolitan song. This musical transition was one of the most incongruous Rich had ever heard, though he knew the Italian piece had to do with Vesuvius, therefore with smoke.

Simonetta looked askance at the performer. "Let's take our plates to another room. I want to tell you about Uncle Leo. The full story. Well, sort of. Nobody knows the *full* story. I see my mom and dad have shown up. I'll introduce you to them later."

Introduce. Mom and dad. Introduce.

"My mother loves old movies, like you do."

Mom and dad. Introduce.

"Dad heads the textile company mom's family started. I told you about the business, right?"

Rich felt the pores in his face and forehead open up, squeeze out tiny dew beads. He swiped his brow with his cotton napkin, which in his mind immediately turned into Ottino the Octopus in front of Simonetta's imagined, and imaginarily revolted, parents. "Oh, I'm so sorry," he whispered.

"What did you say?"

"Oh, uh, that Dalí exhibit sounds good."

As they left they heard Leo call out to the piano player, *"Che cazzo stai suonando!"* (What the fuck are you playing!)

They sauntered through a series of frescoed rooms and marble doorways and then took what was to Rich an unexpected passage to a door near the southwest corner of the building.

"Il salone di relax," Simonetta said. "Hold the bottle." She tugged the brass door handle. "You'll like this."

The blue-green subaqueous light of a huge fish tank suffused the small room. Built seamlessly into a wall, it shone in half a dozen porthole mirrors of Byzantine design. A welcome respite from Leo's towering classical taste, the wood-scented chamber embodied the Eastern legacy of Venice: damask wallpaper dark bluish green with interlacing arabesques and shiny gold filaments; four pint-sized pendant lamps with creamy orange glass windows; a mountainously cushioned sofa in the veined Venetian colors of chrysoprase and porphyry that was fit for a minor seraglio.

"Bella camera," Rich cooed.

"My mother does interior design. This is hers."

"Veramente bella."

"I know you like dim light, colored light. We can sit on the sofa here and use the coffee table. Move what's-his-bust to the side so we'll have more room."

"I think it's Hermes, Greek god of all kinds of crap."

"God of fine perfume."

"Yes, dim light, late-day light," he reaffirmed. "I'm glad you know that. You *know me*. Ever think of how the words for late-day have a kind of thrillingly atmospheric, secretive sound? *Vespro* – or *vespers* in English, which has a sense of the English word *whisper*, which means *bisbiglio* in Italian. *Bisbi*—I like that. The English word *twilight*, which has the French *toi*-sound in it; *twilight* is *crepuscolo* in Italian, another beautiful whispering word."

"You're right. I never thought of that."

"Yes, mostly it's natural light with me, but I must say this fish tank, in this room, has a lot going for it."

She breathed out, squeezed her eyes shut and snapped them open. "I should have brought coffee. Now I'm underrevving."

"I'll go get some."

"No, it's okay." She buried her face in her hands for a moment, looked up at the food. "I'm not even hungry."

"You better eat. You want to get thinner? You're like an eel as it is, especially with those Chinese pants or whatever."

She made a scrunched, laughing face but without a sound.

"A very cute eel, though, with fine tapered ankles."

She went from scrunching to stretching open her mouth and eyes. She shook her head in a silent cry of mock-lunacy and dashed her head into the sofa pillows.

"Simonetta, you are so funny." He thought it was cute the way the sides of her dutch-boy hair whipped left and right. The sight brought the warmth of tears to his eyes, surprising him.

"I'm okay." She straightened up and faced him. "So... Uncle Leo... You know, when you finished talking about deception and all that, remember he said it made him think of, made him nostalgic for, his old profession? Remember the people around him laughed? Well, most of the people who laughed don't really know much about what 'Nico' — that's his old code name — they don't know much about what he was involved in. You probably know almost as much as they do; some idea of a kind of secret service, persuasion, craftiness, all that sort of thing."

"He didn't work steadily for any government, you told me; just helped allied countries at their request, under the table."

"Yes, you won't read about him anywhere. So please, Reech, this is between us. Really. I mean it."

"Of course."

"He was one of the many secret things, sometimes shocking things, new presidents or premiers, you know, leaders of countries, get briefed about when they take office. Briefed, you know, by their absolute top intelligence person. There are probably only two or three people in the world who do what he did, Uncle Leo. He used to build scenarios around people without their knowing it; I mean *mock worlds* costing *millions* in order to alter the outlook of political figures. I mean he would prime them — the target people or persons — it was usually a single person, I think — prime him for use by others, for some other government, who wanted, for example, an agreement, which maybe the target person was not in favor of. You know what I mean? Or it might be to stop the threat of war. He had teams of people working for him, all kinds of connections. It was an agency, like a detective agency; but it didn't uncover things, just did things, made things happen, or not happen. Once, he wired the bedroom of a certain potentate, who was very religious, to play distant sounds—barely audible words—associated with the peace-loving aspects of the person's faith. During the day he arranged it so the guy would encounter omens of different types. And even visions. He used actors, set designs. Once, in order to stop strife within the family of some kind of—I don't know what—an Asian governor or prince, he kidnapped—I mean really kidnapped—two children, one each from the two branches of the family and did *something;* and he brought them back with a message. The shared panic of the families and something to do with the message, whatever it was, brought about the desired situation in the region."

"I mean, these are things I've plucked out over the years. I've never asked him about specific exploits, except when I was a child. You know how children are. But it's more or less quietly understood in the family, built in. Bits and pieces come together, you know, as time passes. You hear this or that."

"Fascinating," Rich said, putting down his fork. "I've suspected there are things like that going on. I mean private people with special skills who are under the radar, so to speak. It's so... Well, it's intriguing to think about. So what are you saying? I mean, do you definitely think he's—"

"He's up to something, yes."

"You really do? But why? I mean, do you actually think he stuck the old guy on the roof to... I don't know."

"Uncle Leo's got a couple of other...aspects. It started when he was a kid, in Bergamo, he and his younger brother, Maurizio, who passed away last July, *buon'anima*. Poor Uncle Maurizio used to head the textile company my great-grandfather started a hundred years ago. There were only two brothers; Uncle Leo was the eldest of six kids; my mother is the youngest. Anyway, simple things, you know, they used to do, the two of them, like nailing their father's slippers to the floor next to his bed and then shouting *fire!* And there were, like, stuffed baby alligators sliding by on strings, a talking dog that scared the hell out of their schoolteacher. They were full of pranks; I mean, you know, two or three times a year they'd pull a prank, and they never grew out of it and the tricks got bigger. A real 'family thing' it was. We expected it. A few years ago, a cousin of ours, who has a place outside Treviso; he was really into UFOs and all that alien stuff, wouldn't shut up about it. Conspiracy buff. Well, Uncle Leo rented a flying saucer-shaped car, a novelty car somebody had; he hired three or four midgets, painted them green..."

Rich, mouth agape, was on the verge of laughter.

"Imagine *that* outside your bedroom window at three in the morning! Flashing lights and all! But this is the purely funny stuff. He does good things, too, always anonymously — that's the way he is; like sending plane tickets to poor folks he had heard about, who couldn't afford to visit their aging parents; he included a letter from Saint Christopher, who wrote that he was pissed off at being de-canonized and wanted to still be involved with travel. Now...the thing is... Sometimes when he gives a gift to friend or a family member, there's a little *adventure* or *puzzle* attached. Know what I mean? Sound familiar?"

"Yes, very familiar."

"So it happened that...all this, you know, turned into his profession, on the world stage."

"On the world backstage, rather. This is great. Thank you. Thank you for telling me. Do you think he..." Rich chuckled "...misses his profession?"

She nodded. "Yes, I'd say so!"

"Sure is terrific material for a story or series. All fiction, I mean. So you think he's...working on an adventure... involving...only us, for some reason?"

She sighed and slid sideways, as if tapped of energy, her head falling into her earlier pillow indentation. She stared at him and said quietly, "He really likes you, Reech."

He scratched an eyebrow. "From what you've told me, I can see how he might have pulled off the old-guy-on-the-roof thing. That's plausible, but..." He frowned and shook his head.

She watched him in silence.

"He called himself Leonardo. Leo? Leonardo? That's curious right there, don't you think?"

Her eyes stayed fastened on him. He detected in her a trace of puzzlement or sadness and he saw himself ignore it. He squinted, licked his lips; he noted her sweet sea-salted perfume. "Yes, the guy on the roof is plausible — *that* I can see after what you told me; but, I was going to say, the kid you gave a lift to, the one with the flaming baby story on the Tron Bridge...that seems to be a real coincidence. You just happened to stop because you thought you forgot your phone, right? I don't know how he could have made that happen." He paused, took a breath, returned her stare, looked away. "At any rate..." He scratched his head and bounced his knee. "It all revolves around the name Tron. I wonder why." He looked at her again; he noticed his anxious knee and checked it. "Did I tell you he held a book too? I *think* it was a book."

She barely nodded.

"I wonder if that has anything to do with anything." He produced a bubbly, ponderous mumble and then stared at the fish tank. "Gosh, they're beautiful, those goldfish. Wow. Fish."

She reached out and cupped his shoulder, shook him slightly in a sympathetic way. As she did so, bells clanged, near and far, clanged familiarly, as if tolling to life the muted detonations now peppering the nighttime.

"Oh," Rich said, "the fireworks have started."

She whispered something. He thought she said, "No fireworks."

He looked at his watch. "Midnight, right on the nose." Tritely he added in English, "How time flies."

They made their way to the roof, where in the days before the building codes, Leo's father, with unquestionable documentation, constructed a low eighteen-columned, terracotta-topped pavilion, which Leo nicknamed the Parthenon. On their way up, Simonetta was mostly silent; she marched behind Rich with her hands on his shoulders, her head pushed against his back, doing a choo-choo train bit. Her ineffable silliness made him smile.

Is she really my girlfriend?

Most of the party had congregated on the roof. He was relieved to hear her parents had left for a midnight concert at Santa Maria della Pietà, a nearby church. Simonetta drifted to the railing and rested her head on her arms like a sleepy child. Prismatic supernovas flashed, exploded, reechoed and then in trembling, falling sparks crackled feebly over the basino, the section of water whose surrounding structures leap out of every Venice picture book: the Ducal Palace, the tidy island of San Giorgio Maggiore with its church and campanile, the fang-end of Dorsoduro with the *Dogana* and the great bulb domes of Santa Maria della Salute. It was one of those moments when Rich thought about his childhood mind and how empty it was *then* of a thrillingly present *now* in the enchanting, improbable city of Venice.

Here I am. How did I get here? Where am I going?

He made one of his stealthy, blindingly fast signs of the cross. He wasn't sure why.

***

Plum pudding.

Rich opened his eyes to the soft red-and-gold-curtained light of morning, glad he had not drunk those eight or ten glasses of champagne he thought he would need.

Budino di prugna.

He reviewed the events of the previous evening. He hadn't broken any mirrors, stepped on anyone's Prada heels, spilled drinks, or made a single stupid comment. He was playful with Leo, he concluded, not insulting.

Plum pudding.

He considered whether his relief at the early departure of Simonetta's parents was foolish. He accepted that it was cowardly, but was it foolish and childish?

Yes, it was.

He flipped over, bunched up his pillow; he closed his eyes and tried to drift away from his thoughts.

"Budino di prugna! Plum pudding!" He sprang up on an elbow, eyes wide. That old man! A few weeks ago! The old man with the plum pudding story! That's who the old guy on the roof looked like. He looked liked the old man with the plum pudding story. Three, four weeks ago. Five weeks ago. *Plum pudding!*

Rich sat up and recalled the day. It was after his first visit to the Fondaco dei Turchi, the massive Veneto-Byzantine shell that houses the Natural History Museum. He wandered round in a dreamy state, exploring the sestiere of Santa Croce. After a spell he found himself in the garden court of the University Institute of Architecture, one of Venice's cloistered, oracle-worthy oases of green. He sat down on a low brick ledge and pored over a few pamphlets he had picked up at the museum.

An old man crept from around a dark corner. He belonged to the "shopping-bag person" category, except that he toted a ripped, rope-bound suitcase instead of a bag. He displayed a week's growth of beard, wore a natty coat, and held a piece of sandwich. Rich recognized the type: He was one of those solitary, benign old souls who haunt urban campuses. He wondered if such men were former professors who, owing to mental or financial hardship, had lost their way in life and now found solace in academic surroundings.

Rich threw himself out of bed and stood still.

What was it? What was the plum-pudding story?

For him, thoughts and thought-developments were real events and a source of popcorn-worthy entertainment. But now his desire for breakfast came up against his blank mental screen, so that this "no-show" condition prevented his enjoyment of food.

So one old man looked like another old man. So what?

He refused to admit that the hint of a further link to the Tron coincidences haunted an outpost of his mind; and, whatever it was, it had to do with plum pudding.

Lemme make a cup of tea.

"Ow!" He slammed straight into the bedroom doorframe. "Dammit!" Weary of translating English *ow's* into Italian *ahi's* (and *achoo's* into *ecci's* for that matter), he resolved to let his native tongue stand alone from now on and went for his glasses among his night-table books.

Plum pudding.

"Jeez."

As he boiled water for tea he realized why he had forgotten the episode. It was the same day his mother, on the phone, let slip that she had been involved in a car accident. It was only a fender-bender, and she was not hurt, but his hearing of it had commandeered his afternoon and obliterated memory of his encounter with the man.

Which reminds me.

He picked up his phone. He spoke to his mother every other day, even if only for a minute. He loved to tell her about Venice and discuss the classic movies they had recently seen.

What am I doing!

He hung up. In his mind, Italy's time zone had entered Rhode Island's. It was one thirty in the morning back home.

I need fresh air.

After only one sip of tea he went to take a shower.

Plum pudding... Plum pudding...

Since he had planned to go out some morning to take photographs, this morning would be good; weather reports promised a clearing of the current grayness. He hoped the tourists and other revelers would be sleeping off the ten days of carnivale. Simonetta, he imagined, was still curled up eel-like under a *frutta di mare* fresco in one of Leo's sumptuous suites.

Out of the shower, he noticed the disk and the secret message on the coffee table, where he had emptied his pockets the night before. "Not now," he told them with a shooing hand, though loose ends made him nervous.

Five minutes later he was out the door.

***

Byzantine windows way, way down, upside down, like pink ribbon-candy quivered, quaked like the old brick walls of raw-meat red, ochre, and burnt sienna; periwinkle sky speckled with floating flora, its fragile clouds ghostly-thin and not quite white; all the bricks and windows repeated and reversed, but solid now and not shivering in the least, stiffly real atop the first and featured scene; while in the middle a slanted mooring post echoed out of its weathered wooden length a wide, off-kilter *V.*

Rich snapped the photo. People should look down more often, he thought, down into the canals. What a world!

He saw the cold morning air glisten behind his face.
Gee I'm feeling better.

He imagined what the Piazza San Marco looked liked this morning; he thought it best to wait a day before going there, give the sanitation people time to whisk the night's festivities into tidy piles and scoop the whole thing up. Yes, the carnival was over: this morning he saw only two leftover celebrants, both in matching costumes (and, he assumed, matching hangovers).

At the Rialto, in contrast, it was more or less business as usual with seabirds swooping, crying, and Venetians going about their morning chores: boatmen calling, merchants unlocking and wiping windows, cranes lifting cages of trash into barges or workers sweeping with medieval-looking twig-brooms. The brighter-eyed tourists snapped take-home photos in the rising sunlight. Rich knew that tight and intricate reflections are not always best in the daytime *Canalazzo*, or Grand Canal, even with its shoulder-to-shoulder *palazzi*. No matter: This morning he needed to face its most recognized span, the Rialto Bridge. He required this view the way people need their morning cup of coffee, his own cup holding a comforting dose of calendar-photo Venice.

Just forget all that plum pudding and Tron stuff.

Before reaching the Rialto, he had mined the Rio di San Luca for double-vaulted reflections of smaller bridges. He took a few shots; then he crossed the Campo Manin, veering to the right and alongside the modern, starch-faced savings bank.

Yuck.

In Campo San Luca, behind the bank, the fresh new sunlight graced the tops of the buildings as people crowded the cafes. He halted to look in the window of the Tarantola bookstore, where he felt a pang for the continual loss of such old-school shops.

His eyes glided from book to book and landed on a monograph about De Chirico. As he eyed the cover he became aware of a person advancing toward him in

47

the window-reflected campo. Without moving his head, he adjusted his stare and focused on the reflection. It was a woman. She was tall and wore a trim, ankle-length black leather coat, dark glasses, and a beret; she held a purse or book. She was headed straight for the window.

Dammit.

He was sure she would stand right next to him.

Dammit.

He detected an adrenaline-circus warming up. To avoid a sweaty silence, he knew he would feel obliged to be sociable and insert a comment beyond the usual *buon giorno*. He couldn't just say *buon giorno* and then scoot away. Or perhaps she would speak first and then he would reply with a dumb, convoluted comment, making a stupid, smiling face.

Oh, the tight-lipped cordial simper!

Already perspiring, he glanced at his watch and turned around, tramping away and looking down as if lost in thought. He wondered why anyone would want to stand next to a stranger at a small shop window if there was no one else right nearby. In her place, he would have loitered discreetly at a distance, waited for the person to finish at the window, and then taken his turn.

But I suppose people are casual like that; fresh-headed, sociable. That's good, I guess. Mom's right. I'm the odd-ball.

Halfway across the campo he glanced over his shoulder with a tourist's broad curiosity to see if in fact the woman went to the window. Yes, she was there — but with her back to it. He stole an extra look, making as if to adjust the strap of his camera bag. She stood still, arms at her side, staring straight ahead as if assessing a track he had left on the pavement.

Whatever.

Now, on the Grand Canal, he considered for the hundredth time the Rialto Bridge, which stood before him. In photographs and at a distance it seemed to be made of light-weight aircraft aluminum or steel. He thought it had a more forward-looking 1930s design than that of a work completed in the last decade of the 1500s. Its style haunted him; he thought he had seen it before in another size and serving another purpose: If one could grab both angled ends and close them together, he mused, one might crack walnuts with it; a mechanic might use it this way to remove lug nuts from wheels (it would make metallic "ratcheting" clicks when opening and closing). Perhaps it could be a staple remover; were it longer, spaghetti tongs.

He climbed the nearly deserted south stair-ramp of the bridge to the apex and gazed south at the great wide-angled highway of luxuriant water, the industrious, millennia-old liquid divide which two sedentary parades of earth- and fruit-toned palaces hem in on both sides. The slanted, crisping, winter-morning radiance—so familiar, like so many forms of light throughout his life—at once silvered and stilled his veins with the deep, solitary, thrilling, and slightly scary sensation of being in and knowing well a fabled place so far away from home.

He raised his camera and took a photo, the same throw-away snapshot he took dozens of times before. Lowering his lens, he again noticed the woman in the trench coat. She strode along the fondamenta, on the bridge-side of the vaporetto stop.

Whatever.

Furthermore (his speaking-thoughts went on), the farther away from home the more wonderfully familiar, in a wide way, the world can seem. This is because of light. If light is the carrier of the practical information that binds us (a tie to be broken only if one of us travels as fast as it), light as an aesthetic or spiritual perception not only rounds out physical objects but washes the moment large with one's forgotten and half-forgotten yesterdays, whispering the unremembered tone of one's life into the present with both a kissed expansiveness and the confident, ineffably blended particulars of a world without end. Painfully beautiful, this is super-time, Eternity in miniature. And we love it, find it sweet, because we love life; we love ourselves and those close to us who came through it with us, now that we sense the whole of it at once. There is no better way to know the present, or to live.

Oh crap, she's coming up the stairs.

Furthermore, weather, especially the change of seasons —

Of course, she's going to stand right here.

Weather, especially the change of seasons, the recurrence, carrying times past, intensifies. Late-day light is best.

That's all. I've lost my thought-flow.

Instead of proceeding down the south side of the outer ramp, he spun around and went under the arch; he crossed the center stairway and stole to the north side of the bridge. Out of curiosity he wanted to see whether the woman would again take the very spot he had occupied. Self-concealment was easier, as merchants on the bridge arranged their shops for the day ahead and more strollers wandered about. He stepped behind the north arch, out of her possible line of vision, but kept one fish-eye goggling at his former post on the other side of the bridge.

He laughed at himself. "What a loon."

The nine o'clock bells of Saint Mark's rang buttery in the distance; a solitary bell north of the bridge followed.

Oh, there she is.

She did not even glance at the canal. Her back to the white stone balustrade, she looked in front of her and down the south ramp several times with flitting, impatient movements.

Rich felt his skin tighten.

God, she...she's actually...!

She scuttled partway into the store-lined center ramp of the bridge and looked left and right down it.

She's gonna come here next. One, two, three, four...

Counting footfalls, he sprinted down the forty-one steps of the north stairs and hid behind the side wall of the first shop. He was sure he had made it there without her seeing him.

Just what the hell am I doing?

He peeked up the central ramp. He darted back and peered around the wall at the steps he descended.

Where'd she go?

From his present post he kept an eye on the visible lower part of the central ramp.

If she wants something, why didn't she stop me?

After a minute she still had not shown herself, and he thought perhaps she had retreated in the opposite direction.

What the hell. This is crazy.

He strode toward the central stair-ramp and was two steps away from entering when she cut in front of him, ambling down. He scraped to a stop and flattened his back against the wall. She strolled unrushed, arms loose, looking straight ahead.

Well, two can play this game.

He let her advance about fifty paces on the Ruga dei Oresi, a corridor of souvenir kiosks beginning at the foot of the bridge. His shadow before him, he followed her with relaxed resolve but unclear purpose. He would not commit to an encounter; but the experience of an event in the making—of a situation that would probably never happen—excited him.

I like it. The gravid emptiness, emptiness trembling with...

Broad contentment, stillness, soothed him. He knew what brought it on; it was the movements he had made up and down and across the bridge. He loved the structure of his escapade; it reflected his poems and other attempts at creative writing. He would love to compose a book that followed a person through corridors, through rooms, up and down spiral stairways, around secret bends, each space fascinating, each with diverse and exotic panoramas now and then from unusual windows.

I love it, but who would read it?

He suspected his early musical background had instilled in him this love of living shape and structure.

Uh oh, where's she headed?

The woman turned in front of San Giacomo di Rialto, said to be the oldest church in Venice and whose huge twenty-four-hour clock reminds one that "time is money," the Rialto having been the center of business from early in the city's history. She crossed the campo diagonally; then she passed under the corner-point of the long line of arches and through the sheltered passage to Campo Cesare Battisti.

Couldn't a corridor, a room, a grove of trees be music? Isn't walking through such structures a musical experience?

His trailing of the woman went in and out of his awareness; and he found himself reviewing his past in relation to the free-and-easy, recreational structure of his current movements.

There was music, yes, and then there were mansions.

Having grown up in Middletown, Rhode Island, he took as his childhood playground the adjacent city of Newport; and he spent half his boyhood bike-riding around this ocean-town of mansions, up and down Bellevue Avenue, hiking Cliff Walk, stopping on the great green lawns spread out behind the Gilded-Age citadels. Big old houses were in his blood; and in an earlier time — a time he hoped would return — they lent an immortal joy to his nighttime dreams.

Imagine wandering in a mansion with countless rooms.

The woman skipped to one side to avoid rolling potatoes from a broken bag a vendor had emptied; and Rich, closer now, made with a dicey piece of footwork to avoid their path and her line of vision.

We're here already?

They had passed through the lively atmosphere of the open-air *erberia* or greengrocery market. The pavement became wet; and the familiar Rhode Island smell of fresh seafood made it morning at the ocean as they headed for the many-arched, red-awning'd fish market loggia or *pescheria*. He thought it would be interesting to pass her to see if he elicited a reaction. Should she enter the pavilion, he would pretend to examine the day's catch, in full view of her. As he closed the distance between them he saw it was not a purse she held but an oversized paperback with a white cover and red letters.

I wonder what she's reading these days.

53

He came up close behind her to the right as she entered the dim, crowded market with its rows of lighted stainless steel tables mounded with crushed ice and lounging sea creatures. Her hand and wrist covered the title of the book, but he could read the author's name in red at the top — *Carl Jung*.

So she's into Jungian Psychology. How interesting.

All at once he froze; a rush of barely born sense made his face visible to his mind as his outward stare locked on the popping eyes and open mouth of a large sea bass.

Omigod! Carl Jung! Plum pudding!

He saw himself spin around, dance away from a near-collision with a monstrous fish on a trolley and then scramble back through the fruit and vegetable tables, his mindless eye skipping from one salad component to the next: broccoli, squash, tomatoes, lettuce, peppers...

Plum pudding!

He slowed under the rear portico of the Fabbriche Nuove, the Sansovino edifice that houses the law courts. He emerged on the Grand Canal, where he backed against the corner arch and stared at the passing streamlined gondolas.

Take it easy. Take it easy. Let me see now... Okay...

Though he detected a nervous reluctance to do so, he tried again to review what the old "plum-pudding man" said to him that day in the courtyard. Was it a dream? The man sat on his well-stuffed valise near Rich and out of the blue brought up "Carlo" Jung, the famous Swiss psychologist.

Yes yes yes...

He spoke in a strained voice with a rough Venetian accent, which made him hard to understand. His nibbling on a sandwich made it even harder. Rich thought he gathered that the man had known Jung, been an assistant or pupil of his.

Yes yes yes...

Like most students of the humanities, Rich had some grasp of Jung's theories, though his knowledge did not go much beyond the widely read popularization of his work *Man and His Symbols.* Besides having coined the terms *introvert* and *extrovert,* Jung was most famous for his investigations into the collective unconscious, the part of the psyche that all humanity shares and whose elements appear cross-culturally in religions, myths, art and dreams (myths, Jung believed, were collective dreams).

Let me see...

Now as he gazed out over the canal, he felt his early unreachable idea was on the verge of connecting with the Tron-coincidences that had haunted him the evening before. He would have to check the Internet to sharpen the particulars of Jung's plum-pudding tale, which the old man had hastily related and which Rich now faintly recalled having read a long time ago.

His back against the arch, he slid down to the cold, hard pavement, took out his Smartphone, and got on the Web. He searched *Carl Jung Plum Pudding.* Instantly he found what he was looking for. The story came from the memoirs of the nineteenth-century poet Émile Deschamps. Jung used it to illustrate his concept of synchronicity, which involved coincidences.

Omigod, that's it. Coincidences without apparent cause.

He took off his glasses, turned his phone horizontally, brought it close to his face, and read:

In 1805 a stranger named Monsieur de Fontgibu treated fourteen-year-old Deschamps to a delicious plum pudding. Fully ten years later, at dinner in a Paris restaurant, the poet requested this specialty for dessert. A waiter told him that another customer had ordered the last plum pudding. This customer was Monsieur de Fontgibu. Seventeen years after this event he was served plum pudding at the home of friends. After relating the early plum-pudding coincidence, he added, "All that is missing is Monsieur de Fontgibu." Suddenly, there was a knock on the door. It was Monsieur de Fontgibu, very old and on the verge of senility. He was searching for an address and had come to the wrong house.

He cradled his face in his hands, rubbed his eyes, kept his face covered. Okay, so... Weeks ago an old man tells me a tale about coincidences, ones that involve plum pudding; he's an old man who just so happens to look a lot like an old man who is part of a series coincidences himself, but ones involving the name *Tron.* And now a woman with a book by Carl Jung...

He looked up at the canal, which resembled a watercolor-wash without his glasses, and lowered his fingers to his lips. Again he wondered how Leo could possibly be behind this.

Am I losing my mind?

He took stock of other memorable coincidences, common ones from his past. Of course, there were the familiar cases which involved thinking about or mentioning a person he had not seen in a long time and then encountering this person on the street the next day. And there was the grandfather clock that stopped when his great-grandfather died. Most frequently he had experienced fortunate research-related coincidences, a lot of those.

Then there were the three dead rodents. One of his young cousins had a hamster that died. A day or two later, the pet white mouse of another relative passed away. Rich joked to his mother that since "death comes in threes" we could expect another rodent, somewhere nearby, to bite the dust soon. That same day the reliable old mouse of his desktop computer quit working and he needed to buy a new one.

A brow of gray clouds moved over the canal and brought back the stony, closed-castle look of winter.

God, even the weather's weird, ass-backwards. Hey, the carnival is over!

He stood up and looked toward the pescheria, where he last saw the trench-coated woman. He did not know what to make of the situation: The appearance of Jung's name seemed purposed to force him to recall what he tried to remember earlier that morning. He wondered what the woman would have said to him. Did she want him to see the book and start a conversation? This was the most likely theory. But what is she up to?

I'll have to call Simonetta. She'll have to call Leo. He can't be doing all this.

With a calmer curiosity, he threaded back through the erberia and into the covered daylight of the pescheria. *"Giorno meraviglioso oggi!"* (Marvelous day today!) a fishmonger broadcast about the morning's catch. Rich stood in one spot and scanned the patrons as they browsed about or made their selections, the dealers weighing their fish and announcing the prices. The mysterious woman, as he expected, was gone. He felt a pinching at his elbow. "Hello?" he blurted, and spun around—eye to eye with a creeping out-of-season crab.

***

"This is Greek and how they spelt her: alpha, beta, gamma delter... *Delta*, I mean."

Seated at his work-dining table, head in hands, he tried to get his bearings with the classical Greek alphabet, which he had not used in years. Though he understood only a smidgen of Greek, he knew how to pronounce and write the words. Yet even with his surface comprehension he saw that the typed words of the message, while made up of Greek letters, were something other than Greek:

ΡΦΧΛΨΗ ΩΛΙΨΛΑΗ ΚΟ ΡΛΦΤΗΨΚΦ ΑΨΦΤ
Ψοχφνη Αψη Ο Ωλιβλιαο:

Χολαψφ Αψηκφτοπφ
Φψωφ Χηψαλποχημοφ
Χολαψφ Αψοβνφ
Αψοβνφ Σλσφ
Χολαψφ Φψωλφρφ ΙΙ
Κφσλτοπφ Γρηθφτοπφ
Γοαηρ Σοπορ Ι
Γοαηρ Σοπορ ΙΙ

As he expected, the text was incoherent; he would have to employ the cipher disk to convert it into an understandable message. Apart from the ancient Greek letters, this decoding activity was familiar to most school children: the substitution of the letters of the inner wheel with those of the fixed outer wheel. There was only one problem: No decoder key or keys accompanied it. A recipient of a secret message, who possessed a cipher disk, must know the secret letter or keyword, must know which letter stands in for the letter *a* and so forth relative to the outer wheel to operate the letter-substitution scheme.

He sat up, tossed his glasses on the table, and pressed the heels of his palms against his eyes. He leaned back, took in air and let it out. He reached for his pack of cigarettes. The episode of the Trench-Coat Lady and the Jung book had given him a reason to renew the pacifying indulgence of tobacco use.

And here it is Lent. Yes, everything's ass-backwards.

He made a cross of ashtray ash on his forehead and blew a stream of smoke to the beamed ceiling. He sipped his cold leftover tea, nibbled at stale galani pastries, and lit up.

So what clue is there? Which letters become what letters?

Though his capacity for math — multiplication in particular — collapsed in the third grade, when his parents were divorced, his aptitude with logical puzzles was exceptional. He felt a hypnotic and nearly unlimited confidence in his ability to conquer them.

So we need a third thing, don't we? The key. They gave us the message, the wheel, and the...what? What's the keyword...? The keyword... What's the keyword...?

Smoothing his eyelids, he stood up and plodded toward the three steps that led down to the living-room area.

Sonafabitch!

He slipped at the top step to avoid the wayward lamp cord and slid down on his side, catching the delicate, flickering fixture. On his back, eyes wide, he studied the ceiling.

"Tron!" he exclaimed. "That's it, you stupid ass!"

Back at the table he hypothesized that *t* or *tau* (τ) of the inner wheel would become *a* or *alpha* (α) of the outer wheel so that the letter following τ, which is upsilon (υ), would become beta (β), the second letter of the alphabet, and so forth. He recalled that Leo — "Aha!" — knew he was familiar with Greek; the subject of ancient alphabets had come up during the dinner they had at Antico Martini months earlier.

Oh yes, this is one of his games.

He rotated the *T* of the inner wheel, positioning it under the *A* of the outer wheel and proceeded from there. If he did not understand the Greek it would be an easy matter to figure it out with a dictionary or find a person who knew the language. For the first word, he arrived at ΛΟΠΕΡΑ. He pronounced it: "loh-*per*-rah." It sounded only vaguely Greek.

He pronounced it a few times and then started on the second word. He came up with ΣΕΓΡΕΤΑ *and* pronounced it: "seh-*greh*-tah."

What a minute... This is Italian!

The first word was pronounced *loh*-per-rah. It was "L'OPERA" meaning *the work* or *the opera*. The second word was ΣΕΓΡΕΤΑ, meaning *secret*. *L'OPERA SEGRETA* or THE SECRET WORK. He continued; he completed the first line: ΛΟΠΕΡΑ ΣΕΓΡΕΤΑ ΔΙ ΛΕΟΝΑΡΔΟ ΤΡΟΝ or THE SECRET WORK OF LEONARDO TRON.

Leo, you clever bastard.

The second line came out as *Riposa Tra I Sequenti* or *Rests Among The Following.*

He kept on deciphering. Χολαψφ became Πιετρο and this became *Pietro* or, in English, *Peter*. Then Αψηκφτοπφ became Τραδονικο and this became the

Italian surname *Tradonico*. He had read books on Venetian history and knew that Pietro Tradonico was an early doge. The text needed a couple of minor transliteration adjustments, but a half an hour later he possessed the full, clearly written text:

THE SECRET WORK OF LEONARDO TRON
Rests Among The Following:

Pietro Tradonico
Orso Partecipazio
Pietro Tribuno,
Tribuno Memo
Pietro Orseolo II
Domenico Flabonico
Vital Michiel I
Vital Michiel II

"Okay..." So what is the secret work and where do these doges rest? They're entombed all over the place. A hundred and twenty of them, right? Of course, these are probably in one spot—I hope. "Leonardo... Secret work." The old man on the roof called himself Leonardo and held some kind of book. Secret work?

He put on his glasses, lit another cigarette, stood up. He planned to call Simonetta to tell her about the plum-pudding episode and now the message; but first he went over to his stacks of books on the floor and looked through the indexes of several histories of Venice, searching for references to Leonardo Tron. He found a lot about Niccolò Tron, the sixty-seventh doge, whose likeness appeared on the first Italian coin to be called *lira*, the *Lira Tron*, in 1472. He had his profile stamped on the coin, a practice that went against the

Most Serene Republic's sensibilities. (Rich wondered why he did it, as he was such a dull-looking, liver-lipped cuss.) The doge refused to trim his beard, letting it grow as a memorial to his dead son, whom he loved very much. He noted lesser though important officials from the patrician Tron family: Andrea, an ambassador; another Andrea, diplomat; another Niccolò, ambassador; there was a Giovanni, a Pietro, a Girolamo (executed as a traitor). He saw no Leonardo.

Back at the table, he lit another cigarette. He sensed the colorful fragments of a palace—the situation-pieces of a story-castle—dance around him, but with missing bricks and scarce instructions for its assembly. He picked up his phone to call Simonetta, flung a scarf around his neck and went out onto the long, narrow terrace, whose single door was beside his table.

A story castle...

The smell of cooking tomato sauce and garlic rose from below. His mother's kitchen flashed through him.

Simonetta, I deciphered the message!

He blew a matching cloud into the grayish sky as a solitary pigeon cooed above his head.

"A story-castle," he hushed. He liked the image, as if a castle or mansion could be assembled from the pieces of a story. What would it be like? The idea stilled him, the way he loved to be stilled; it opened him up for musing, for his inner Marco Polo, to the point where almost nothing else mattered.

Simonetta, I deciphered...

On fine days he saw clearly the upper extremities of the houses on the other side of the Grand Canal, but now only a line of ghostly box-tops trimmed the distance beyond the terracotta foreground roofs. Though the effects of winter light were often wondrous, overcast days yielded only a couple of "mansions" to go to. Lonely and thrilling, often achromatic and enclosed, such days were a little extra scary. They stopped time, but in the narrow present; they brought only a trickle of the "here-there-and-everywhere" of time's huge "mansion" with its mix of countless places, in its flecked and inexpressible amplitude, which in a series of light-blessed days his poetry thrived on.

He thumbed through his phone's small database of numbers until he reached Simonetta's. He stared at it.

But that's the thing about melancholy weather, isn't it?

An image came to him of Simonetta's apartment, which he had never been to: they sit relaxed on a soft leather chesterfield, side by side, reading Saint Augustine's *Confessiones* and dreaming of the North African sun, which the blazing fireplace and their casually converging limbs make real against the purgatorial day.

Yes, *that's the thing, isn't it? Why people hook up. The protection. The buttressing. Then, of course, there's the burrowing.*

The swampy, dismal and unplumbed depths of the teeming, vaporous lagoon with its cryptic, pestiferous isles of bones and forsaken, screaming asylums; the incremental dissolution of Venice herself, as people and their personal epochs the world over likewise slip away, inexorably sink toward their death—all of this prods the living soul toward the conservation of life.

And the creation of new life.

His finger rubbed the *send* icon on his phone.

Yes, yes, of course, this is what's going on.

He snuffed out his cigarette and slid his phone in his pocket. A possible partial answer to the Tron mystery was coming into focus. He had half suspected that it was an attempt by Leo to fashion an adventure for him and Simonetta. But, aware of his tendency to miss or repress social tiff-offs, he had fled the sharper reason: Leo, in short, was a crafty, grandiose matchmaker.

He grasped the wrought-iron railing to re-test its strength and leaned forward against it. It all added up: Leo was out to create a bond between him and Simonetta.

Sure, a mad bachelor who mixes the DNA of others.

And it was all by way of a fun exploit, in his trickster fashion. With sudden clarity he considered what she said to him about Leo: *"He really likes you, Reech."*

I guess he thinks I'm a fine young man. Gosh. And Simonetta calls me sweet names. I don't catch on. Am I a dope or what?

He went back inside and dropped himself onto the sofa. Curling up, he wandered the magical geometries of the oriental carpet and then gazed up at the gray-day windows.

But (he hypothesized), after the cold, leaden era, which her presence relieved, a conducive, luminescent epoch would return; hundreds of his personal "here-there-and-everywheres" would blossom in redeeming nanosecond flecks, each crammed with the shock of times and places, all aching for conversion into art, a work fashioned from those speck-hints of Life Everlasting.

Then I'd have to divorce her. Leave her with the kids.

The thought of her natural, childlike winsomeness, however, brought a warm wetness to his eyes. "Little eel," he sighed. He realized the good-girl-bad-girl rumor about her was probably one of Leo's orchestrations designed to worry him or make him jealous. He huffed a resigned sigh. "I dunno."

What difference does it make? I'll be out of money in a month or two and back in Rhode Island looking for a job.

He shrugged himself off the sofa, returned to the table, and picked up the decoded message.

Leo's made tomb-hunters of us now. Gotta find out where these doges are holed up.

He marched toward to his books but hesitated. No, he decided, the coincidental events were too wide-ranging for anyone to engineer. Or were they? *"The Secret work of Leonardo Tron,"* he murmured as if pronouncing the title would provide an answer. Then he emitted one of those hard-to-define Italian sounds: *"Boh."* He took out his phone to call Simonetta, but the angry buzz from the apartment's intercom made his finger freeze on the *Send* icon. His heart dropped at the thought of social intercourse with a total stranger.

On unnecessary tiptoes he hurried to the front door and hesitated at the responder box. This was one of the few times someone used his buzzer. His name was not on the brass button-plate outside.

He pushed the *respond* button. "Yes, who is it?"

The male voice grunted abruptly, paused. "I am looking for..." A second of silence followed his poor, heavily accented Italian. "Leonardo Tron."

He felt his face glow and his heart pick up speed.

"Jesus, Mary, and Joseph," he mouthed. He pushed the button. "Who?" he asked. He wanted to hear the name again.

"Le-o-nar-do Tron."

"No, no such person here. Sorry."

He dashed to the front windows and looked down into the courtyard. As usual, he saw no one. Most of his neighbors worked during the day, and two in his building were summer-only residents, so the zone was quiet. The courtyard was small, around twenty paces by ten; houses almost completely surrounded it. He waited a minute. No one moved away from the building.

Maybe I should go down. Yes, let's confront this thing.

He threw on his coat and with echoing footsteps trotted down four flights in the dim light of the stairway. Reaching the *pianterreno*, an archaically tiled entrance area, he unlocked the heavy wooden double door and pushed it partly open.

He looked right and left, close to the building; then he ambled to the center of the cortile. The only way in and out of the courtyard was a narrow passage, five or six paces long, beside the side wall of San Beneto; then it turned right for several meters and opened into the campo in front of the church.

All at once voices flared in the reverberating passage, voices speaking, colliding; then a man's shout, a woman's, a burst of abusive cries; then scuffling, thumping, and grunting exclamations. Rich scampered cautiously to the opening of the corridor. Conscious of his body, he inched in closer to peer around the bend. A short, stocky man, who appeared Asian, and a tall, thin woman struck each other and blocked each other's blows. The woman had the upper hand with a rolled-up pocket umbrella. She knocked his sunglasses off and whacked the sides of his big bald head. She yanked his red scarf, choking him.

The combatants broke and the man stormed away. Rich tingled all over when he realized the woman was the stalker with the Jung book he had played cat-and-mouse with on the Rialto. "You little shit-ass!" she cried in a British-sounding voice. The man shouted an echoing oath from around the bend. She stayed in place, examining a long torn flap on her coat. She stooped to pick up her hat. Rich scooted back into the building. He kept a thin crack in the front doors, waiting to see if she entered the courtyard.

Look at yourself.

He wondered how Humphrey Bogart would play this part. Jimmy Cagney? George Raft?

Hell, I'm no tough guy.

Cary Grant? Ray Milland? Even Ray would approach her. Begging pardon, he'd want to know what all the fuss was about.

And here I am playing hide-and-seek like Shirley Temple.

He pushed through the doors, marched across the courtyard.

"Let's settle this thing!"

The passageway was empty. The campo beyond was empty. Nobody anywhere. Only the clang of bells disputing the hour.

***

The next morning the bronzed giants of Saint Mark's clock brained their bell as Rich stepped into the vast trapezoid Piazza, home of Venice's wondrous basilica; while on the opposite side of the square, workers in hardhats disassembled the great carnival stage, whose windows still mimicked the box seats of the Fenice Theater. He counted the first bell strike, which meant he had to count the next eight. Does anything, he asked himself, root a person more into a story than church bells? Near and far, the bells of Venice brought to his mind the clangs and dongs in the countless Italian films he watched while growing up, the bells of cities, the bells of hilltop towns.

They bring that far-off stillness.

Then the bells of Mark's tower, rich and delirious, joined in. He thought perhaps Simonetta was right when he eventually spoke to her on the phone the day before: they were involved in a kind of story; they should enjoy it in this vein, as an entertainment, and take note of any further developments.

Okay, maybe.

Both concluded that the two people he saw fighting outside his courtyard were not actors; that "something was up," a shady enterprise neither could interpret. "I only hope there's no danger," he sighed, to which she impertinently answered, "What could eight dead doges do to us?" Using his reference books on Venetian history, he determined that the doges listed in the secret message were entombed in the crypt of San Zaccaria Church. While the church dates from the fifteenth century, it was the original seventh-century structure whose still-surviving crypt received the remains of the eight heads of state listed in the message, beginning with Pietro Tradonico (stabbed to death at the church in the year 864) and ending with Vital Michiel II in 1173 (stabbed to death down the block). Rich had seen the crypt years earlier from a narrow visitor's walkway near the entrance.

Before tackling the tombs, he was to meet Simonetta for breakfast in a place he had never visited, because of the expense: the historic Caffè Florian, in the colonnaded portico of the Procuratie Nuove, whose arches line the fashionable south side of the present piazza. Another sight, however, diverted his visual beeline away from the lavish coffee house: Saint

Mark's Basilica, eccentric queen prickly with ornamental accretions, nesting in her court, must register in his eye no matter how many times he came before it; and he took it in, reformulating, as others had, an analogous idea of the church that went beyond the obvious reflection of Constantinople: Mark Twain famously saw it as a "warty bug" (Rich pictured a camelback cricket); Goethe saw a colossal crab; but to his own mind it was a amalgamation of solidified circus- or carnival tents, the "Big Top" of Byzantium in the West; and he easily imagined its colorful mosaic'd lunettes lacking the relic-adventures of the Evangelist and exhibiting instead Saint Jo-Jo the Dog-Faced, the Bearded Madonna, and, of course, a winged lion and its tamer.

Super-fast he crossed himself. *"Pax tibi Marce."*

"Ciao, tesorinooo!" he heard in the distance. Simonetta, flagging him with both hands, was exiting the Merceria, the ancient shopping street that comes out under the clock tower.

She's right on time. A good trait.

She wore a padded, tight-fitting black parka and a deep violet ski cap that matched her collar lining. Like him, she carried an under-arm briefcase. Hers overflowed with papers.

"Ciao, anguillina!" (little eel), he called to her as she neared him. She shot one of her sharp squeak-laughs, which sounded the way an eel looks. *"Anguillina!* I love it!" She nearly knocked him over as she kissed him on both cheeks. "You called me that the other night. It's funny; my father once called me *bixi*. Ha! *Bixato* is the Venetian word for *eel."* Her face and pink-rimmed nostrils showed a healthy, breathing look of excitement. She patted her case. "I can't wait to show

you what I found! *"Andemo!"* she said in Venetian, meaning *"Andiamo."*

They entered the café, a suite of jewel-box rooms dating from the 1720s. The air was rich, sweet, and creamy with opulent breakfasts of coffees and pastries. A white-jacketed young man with white bow tie, black vest, and black trousers smiled at them.

"Signorina Simonetta, buon giorno. Buon giorno, signore."

"Ciao, Bernardo," Simonetta said, offsetting his formality. Rich reset the tone with his own *buon giorno* and dignified nod.

"By a window, Bernardo."

They followed the waiter out of the central hall through one *sala* and into another, which like the first was ribbed wall-to-wall-to-ceiling with many meters of intersecting gilt wainscoting that outlined everything—frescos, tapestry effects, huge gold mirror. Rich felt he was inside an outside-in Eighteenth-Century music box. They sat on red velvet, she with her back to the window, he at her right facing the entrance to the room. In flurry of words, she gave their order.

"Okay, Reech..." She lowered her voice, business-like and private, since two other couples occupied the room. She unfolded, opened and refolded a copy of *Il Gazzettino*, a popular and partly sensational regional paper. "Look at this. I skipped right over it the first time. You know you were in the news?"

He winced as he took the paper and focused on the short article under her deep-violet fingernail. Its headline was a takeoff on the title of a musical work by Arnold Schoenberg—*Transfigured Night*—an allusion he found surprisingly recherché for this newspaper:

NOTTE TRASFIGURATA O NO?

The last night of the carnival saw a number of emergency calls, all bearing an element of fantasy. In one instance, a young American man, on extended stay in this city, claimed to see on his roof an old man dressed in ancient garb. He reportedly had a bloody face and held a torch, which, in the opinion of the witness, posed a fire hazard, even though the flame, the witness admitted on reflection, may have been fake.

Rich stopped reading, rolled his eyes, and took a breath. Simonetta's single sharp laugh pierced his eardrum, made heads turn. She cupped her mouth with her hand. He resumed reading.

Another person, a teenage boy from Milan, said he saw a baby on fire in a window near the Tron or Piavola Bridge. In a fit of excitement the boy vomited on police officer Gagliardi. In a third case, a female resident of the Santa Croce district called the police when she was frightened by "a growling monster with really big teeth" sitting on an arch near her home in Calle dei Albanesi. The witness thought it was "some kind of lion or tiger or bear."

Investigation yielded no evidence in support of the claims. In two instances alcohol and possibly drugs may have been involved, but mischief has not been ruled out. As always authorities ask the public to avoid unnecessary emergency calls, as they may interfere with persons in legitimate need of assistance.

Both were silent as their fruit, croissants, biscotti, coffee, and tea arrived on a two-tiered silver server.

Rich groaned. "I could have been deported."

"You see there's a third person who saw something weird. The Santa Croce girl. Says she saw a monster."

"What's that about?"

She held up a spiced almond biscotto. She shoved it in the corner of her mouth like a cigar and with both hands pulled from her case several disarranged sheets of paper. She thrust them at him. They were photocopies of reports, police reports.

"Where did you get these?"

"I know some people at the *questura* over here."

"Who *don't* you know?"

"The girl's name is Ornella Riusi. She lives with her sister and her sister's husband. Look at the top page. See the street name they put down? You read it in the article."

"Calle dei Albanesi."

"Right. Now the arch she says the monster was sitting on is at the end of her street. I looked it up. You know what the intersection is, the name of the other street? Can you guess?"

He was quiet for a moment. "Okay," he chuckled, "let me see..." He pretended to think. "Sounds like...*Tron?*"

Simonetta stretched open her mouth, wrinkled her nose, and squinted at him. Her face resembled a piece of popcorn.

Rich snorted and shook his head. "Simonetta, this is getting scary. This is really getting scary, Simonetta."

"It's another Calle Tron. And, you know, you didn't say anything and I didn't say anything either when we spoke on the phone, but the place where you said you met the old 'Plum Pudding Man' that day..."

He bit his lip and looked at the floor, nodding.

"You know that's the courtyard of the Palazzo Tron."

"I repressed it," he admitted. "Sure, it's the architecture and design institute. I know it, knew it." He looked down, squeezed his hands between his thighs, and hunched his shoulders.

"Aw, *poveretto*" (poor little thing), "don't be afraid!"

"I'm not afraid."

"Here, look up, *mangia, mangia!*" She grabbed a croissant and drilled it into his mouth. "Bite, bite, bite!"

His chin and shirt covered with flaky crust, silent laughter commandeered him as he brushed the bits off his sweater.

"*Bravo ragazzo!*" (Good boy!)

It was one of those inexorable laughs, which made him see his face as a jagged, disjointed portrait by Picasso; he thought it a form of hysteria and, making it worse for himself, tried to hide it from the other patrons. It was no use: a self-scourging part of him further fueled his spasms by injecting into his mind a few of the cafe's most famous patrons—Casanova, Dickens, Balzac, Hugo, Proust, Stravinsky, and a posturing band of Italian independence fighters—each watching him with the gravest distain.

"Oh brother," he groaned in English, wiping his eyes. "Victor Hugo with that mushy beard!"

"What?"

"Nothing."

"I love it when I make you laugh like that. It's good. We're going to need a sense of humor when we go down into the crypt."

"Down into the— Oh yeah. I repressed that too."

Rich paid for breakfast. It was not distressingly expensive since the small orchestra was not playing, as it does beneath the outside arches when the al fresco tables are set up for business.

Simonetta stopped short in the slanted morning light of the piazza. "You know, I should have brought my *acqua alta* boots. The crypt gets flooded, no? We had acqua alta a few days ago."

"You mean you think we'll have to actually go into it, really in, I mean past the entrance?"

"I don't know. Could be."

"I guess I assumed Leo would hide the book, or whatever it is, near the stairway. I'm trying to recall what it was like. Do you think he'd really want us to walk into the water?"

"Well, it's not like it would be up to our waist. Listen, don't you fret over it your usual way. I'll do it."

"I've got boots too, at home. I can do it. Do I fret?"

"Come home with me. I've got the gondoletta."

I'll see what her place is like.

They ambled along the north side of the basilica and into the Calle de Canonica, a lane leading to the canal of the same name. Steps later they saw the back of the Ponte dei Sospiri, or Bridge of Sighs, the elevated limestone corridor behind the Doge Palace; from the narrow passage prison-bound convicts would take their final look at the outside world. A perturbed element in Rich, involving the adventure in which he found himself, smoked his spirits with a touch of the prisoner's mood.

Yeah, I do fret. Enjoy yourself dammit! This is fun!

Looking up at the bridge, he recited with forced sentiment Lord Byron, who gave the structure its popular name: "I stood in Venice, on the Bridge of Sighs; a palace and a prison on each hand." Simonetta chortled; but he thought of Byron's bouts with melancholy; how he swam the whole Grand Canal, starting at the Lido, the exercise providing relief from his darker states.

I should learn how to swim. Play tennis. Something.

The gondoletta was parked by the Museo Diocesano, across the canal.

Didn't Byron drown?

The museum hosted the Salvador Dalí exhibit and displayed on its façade a large blue and yellow poster of the artist, who looked down on Simonetta's peculiar boat with a blend of affronted and scheming regard. Rich thought he saw in him a touch of envy too; for as the whimsical craft sailed away the thrill of again experiencing Venice as it was originally meant to be lived made him feel blessed with good fortune. He thought he would like to spend a year knowing the city exclusively from its aquatic perspective as one knows the asphalt turns of one's hometown.

They passed beneath two of the three closely spaced bridges, floating smoothly through the age-seasoned corridor of windows, arches, and balustrades, waving back at grinning gondoliers and catching the eyes of tourists whose charmed glances changed places with smiling mouths as they lifted their cameras. Then, as they approached the third bridge—

"Simonetta, look down!" He pointed to the water.

"What is it?"

He encircled her with his arms, sheltering her; he steered her head and shoulders. "Look down into the water. Over there."

"What? What is it?"

In a moment the bridge darkened the day.

"Okay, look straight ahead now." He kept one arm around her, their heads together, hand on hand, like classic lovers on a gondola ride. The boat, traveling admirably straight as ever, floated back into daylight.

"Keep looking ahead."

"What is it, Reech? What did you see?"

He relaxed and released her, briefly noting the uncomforting loss of their physical connection. "On the bridge. It was that guy. Don't turn around. I'm almost certain. The Chinese guy, Asian guy, whatever, who was fighting with the woman outside my place. Same bald head, red scarf. He was looking at a map."

"Do you think he knows us? You sure it's him?"

"I don't know. I just didn't want him to see us. Maybe it was him. I don't know." He whistled a sigh. He slid his arm around her again and cupped her nearest shoulder with his other hand, bracing and then releasing her. He pondered the need to squeeze her more indulgently. "I could be wrong. Maybe it was just a tourist. Lots of Chinese in Venice these days."

They turned left after the bridge and in thoughtful silence continued on the same rio for about ten minutes, completing a long, irregular arc. She pointed. "I live over here."

"Wait, I know this spot. So this is where we are. Ha! This is Marco Polo's neighborhood."

"Right. His house was where the Malibran Theater is. The newer wall there with the windows has a plaque on it."

It was an intimate spot with a red white-trimmed brick bridge that leaped diagonally across the narrow canal; a geometric wrought-iron rail trimmed the short fondamenta.

"It took me awhile to find this spot on my first trip to Venice. There are these Byzantine arches in the courtyard on the other side there. He must have walked under those many times — when he was home."

She moored the boat and they passed through the dark, chilly *sotopòrtego* that tunneled to the exemplary Venetian courtyard with its crowded, eclectic collection of windows, dark green shutters, doors, arches, and architraves all set into walls of ancient bricks. He wondered what her place was like, what signs it would emit. Was she messy? Neat? Funky?

Funky? No way.

Through double wooden doors they entered a small foyer. Heavy looking Spanish furniture sparsely bedecked it; and a mystical geometry of Moroccan tiles blanketed the floor. Lacy black sconces resembling fancy fans gave off triangular shapes of light on the pale green walls. The space reminded him of a miniaturized version of a lobby in an old American movie palace.

"*Ben fatto*" (well done), he said.

Up three flights of less adorned stairs, they stopped at her black-lacquered door. It was slightly ajar. She gave him a quick surprised look. "Don't tell me I forgot to lock it again."

They listened for interior noises. "It's probably okay," she murmured, and they glanced at each other questioningly. Inside, she scanned the wide space with its high ceiling and expanse of hardwood floors. The furniture, Rich noted, was neither too modern nor too "period"; it was stylish and tasteful in a basic twentieth-century way. All was acceptably neat, he thought, for a girl.

"*Bello*," he repeated. "Nice place."

"Everything seems okay. Nothing out of order, I don't think. My violin is still there."

"You play the violin?"

"Wait a minute."

"I play the lute. But not for a year now."

She walked over to a drafting table that functioned as a desk and looked on it and all around it. Then she lifted her briefcase to her eyes and stirred the pages in it. With a puckered brow she scanned the room again."

"Everything okay?"

"When we were talking on the phone yesterday I made notes. I wrote down what the message said, what you told me, *The Secret Work of Leonardo Tron* and the names of the doges and all the rest. *San Zaccaria crypt.* I wrote it with a big black marker on a sheet of printer paper. I left it on the desk. Right there all by itself."

They stared at each other again.

"I'll get my boots."

He was aware that they both were reluctant to mention the man they had just seen on the bridge. He could not determine whether his own reticence was out of the fear of appearing conspiratorial and "over-the-top," or whether it was from the fear of fear itself, or whether it was a matter of simple denial.

Over-the-top. That's it.

As Simonetta disappeared into another room he listened in that direction for disruptive sounds.

No, it's fear itself.

He pressed a finger to his lips and went to her bookshelves.

Lots of mystery titles. That figures.

Leaping out at him were Conan Doyle, Agatha Christie, Rex Stout; four or five were in English but most were in translation.

No Chesterton, however.

He saw unfamiliar names of Italian mystery writers.

There's simply not enough time to know them.

He went over to a stack of CDs and noted with reassurance that, at first sight, he saw nothing wild or adolescent among the popular music; though one grainy, black and white box cover displayed a scruffy Italian singer, whose overemotional, gravelly voice he thought he could deduce from the look of him.

Oh, Mahler's Fifth, Lorin Maazel conducting. God bless her. Mahler Two, Solti. Nice! Look, there's some Benny Goodman.

With special delight he saw two CDs of Antonio Carlos Jobim and João Gilberto, the Brazilian songwriters. Though his own taste in popular music ended with the big bands of the 1940s, isolating him in this regard from at least two later generations, he had a particular fondness for certain post-1940s Brazilian songs, especially those by Jobim and Gilberto. He loved that sweet, resigned but dreamy longing before the unattainable. He recalled having mentioned this music to her, and wondered if her owning these discs might have resulted from his unintentional recommendation.

He spied a stack of discs on the floor partly hidden beneath a canvas bag. "Oh my gosh!" He ducked at the sound of cascading rubble in the next room. "Everything okay?"

"*Che noia!* I can't find my cheap crinkly plastic boots. Those are the ones I need. The *stivali piaghevoli*" (foldable boots). "They're here somewhere."

He moved over to the windows, which looked down on the little diagonal bridge. The impressionistic tones of a Ravel piano work sparkled nearby and mixed with a gondolier's heartfelt song. He turned away from the windows and sat down on the black leather sofa. He noticed a few of her four-page monthly bulletins — *Venezia mese (Venice Month)*. It listed events by sestiere. Colorful ads brightened it up. Then he focused on a sheet of paper, which lay to one side; the squared-off, right-justified paragraph looked familiar. He fingered it toward him and saw one of his poems, a rare "theoretical" one:

That continuous back-and-forth of the two harmonic steps — near and far — here and there — then and then — with the first a consonance — a rest — and the other a heart-rending blur — a dissonance — a yearning: rest — reaching — rest — aching — rest — in the day — in the heavens — on the mansion lawns above the sea. What is it? Consonance — tender dissonance — consonance — dissonance — the tick and the tock. And out there arching over — unknown as if in the blue of ocean sky — the soundless loving Always. There's no beginning and no end!

"It's out there," he sighed, "near and far, calling. Real Life."

Yes, but...?

He conjured up the soothing, earthly (and therefore competing) feel of Simonetta's darling boney shoulders.

So how could I ever — ?

"I found them!" Simonetta came out, dangling two crumply boots of shiny silver material. "See, they scrunch up and I can stuff them in my case. I've got a nice flashlight too."

Cute how she blinks it on and off.

"And it floats!"

Back in the gondoletta, they made an ungainly K-turn and headed in the direction they came in. "You think we should turn over here instead taking the route we took before?"

Rich made a clueless gesture.

"We've got to go a little east of San Marco. But I'm not sure about this rio. I've never taken it."

"We might go and park where we were before, under Dalí's nose. It's not a long walk to San Zaccaria from there. In fact, it's not a long walk from where we are right now."

"The boat's only for a week. Let's be adventurous."

Rich shot her a dubious sidelong look.

She turned left into the narrow canal; it was picturesque with recessed, bricked-up windows, wrought-iron railings, and the red, blue, and white reflections of a little bridge ahead of them. A few minutes later she was frowning and talking to herself. "Calle de la Nave...Calle del Volto..." She navigated tight, shadowy, sun-striped angles, drifting now and then under snugly hidden bridges; they purred past the cascading winter greenery of time-tinkered windows and the endless species of age-encrusted bricks, shutters, terraces, balustrades, doors, docks, steps, grilles, grates, pipes, rust, peeling plaster scabs, and the mossy, varicolored watermarks on the skin of the houses. "Let's see now..." They made their way into a wider canal. A gondola loaded with smiling Chinese girls waved at them and Rich waved back. "Okay, Santa Maria Formosa's up ahead on our left, the campanile. San Zaccaria is past that to the right."

She heard her phone emit familiar series of *whoops*. "Who's Skyping me?" She pulled her phone from her case, squinted at it, and then cried out the name of the caller: "Dogetradonico864!" She let out a playfully panicked squeak-scream. "Oddio! Look at this, Reech, look at this!" He saw the name. "What! Well answer it!" She fumbled for the answer icon and pushed it. On the miniature screen an old man presented himself in the guise of an ancient doge with full white beard, gold satin raiment and the single-horned cap of his high office. "Get out of my crypt, both of you!" he cried. "Out! Out at once! Let me rest in peace!"

Simonetta let fly a wild eel-squeal into Rich's wide-eyed, open-mouthed face. "Look! Look!"

"What the hell? What's going on!"

Bouncing up and down, she jabbed her finger at the image. "It's the doge! Doge Tradonico!"

"Get out of my crypt!" the man commanded again.

"Simonetta, dead doges don't use iPhones!"

"Out, or I'll hang you both upside down from the two columns, right under the giant perfume ad, after searing your eyes with hot coals of course, for good measure!"

Simonetta leaned forward and made one of her laughing "popcorn" faces, covering her mouth with her hand.

All at once the "doge" looked off-screen and said "What? What?" He frowned. "Oh," he grunted, sounding deflated. Looking back into the camera he made a garbled utterance. Then the screen went black with a resigned *poo-poo-poo* noise.

They looked at each other. "Oh yes! No doubt about it now. It's uncle Leo's doing." She wiped her eyes. "What a crackpot!"

"I don't know what to say."

"I told you he's the consummate prankster!"

Rich rubbed his forehead. "Who was that guy? An actor?"

"No doubt."

"Okay, well, at least now we—"

"There's one thing I don't get." She turned up both hands.

Rich snorted. "Only one thing?"

"Or else he miscalculated. I mean, we're not in the crypt."

"In the—? Oh, I see what you mean."

"That's the thing. The doge was supposed to chase us out of the crypt—isn't that it?—and we're not in there yet."

"Right, it doesn't make sense."

"Something didn't work. I think they realized it all of a sudden. Did you get that impression?"

"Well, yes, the guy seemed to lose it at the end. You want to try calling back to see what happens?"

"No no, the thing isn't over. He put something in the crypt for us to get—the Tron-thing, the book, the secret work."

"You know, I wonder if... No, nothing."

They sailed in suspended silence for a moment past the wide white fondamenta of Santa Maria Formosa.

Simonetta restarted the conversation. "You think... You think something may have been rigged to call my phone, from the crypt?"

"I was going to say... An auto-dialer maybe or some contraption. It could have set itself off by accident or—"

"Right. Well, no matter what, we've got to go down there. After we do, whatever the result, we'll call Uncle Leo to—"

"Round things out."

"—tell us what the story is, but..."

"But what?"

Simonetta sighed, looked Rich in the face, then back at the route. "I don't know what. Let's go see."

Rich clasped himself and drew his knees together.

She confused Campo San Zaccaria with another location and became lost. *"Una deformazione dello spazio"* (a space warp) she theorized. Then it took a half an hour to locate a safe parking spot close to their destination. At last they were striding through Campo San Provolo and into the quiet square of San Zaccaria and its church. The handsome, smooth-shouldered, saintly-white edifice, whose facade soars steeply from Gambello's Gothic polychrome coffers to Codussi's vault-windowed, classic-columned divisions—a house dedicated to John the Baptist's father—stood erect and reserved before them, visually belying its history of partying nuns, whose aristocratic but penniless parents forced them into holy orders.

They passed through the wood-framed vestibule and into the nave. Stained glass windows and flickering votive candles lighted the soundless hollow. What is such a zone, Rich asked himself; what but the interior of a bejeweled womb or the insides of a heavenly brain modeled after an impossibly glorious MRI? He halted to breathe in the hugely delicate, magnificently elaborated space, its walls structured with priceless works of Bellini and others. Five people sat motionless in the pews.

"Reech," Simonetta whispered, noticing he had stayed behind. Her whisper nudged him out of his reverie. She pointed to the right aisle. From there one entered the rooms that led to the crypt. He approached her and noticed she had removed her ski cap, a proper gesture, he thought, especially when standing beneath the angel-hoisted, glass-sided sarcophagus of San Zacharias, said to hold the saint's remains. He whispered, "You think...we should...go ahead with it?"

I mean, you know..." He made a blooming motion with his hands. "Well," she whispered back, "it's not like there are popes or saints down there. They're old dead doges. And, after all, it's way under the church."

No one guarded the entrance to the anterooms, where an attendant often sat to accept the entrance fee. They looked around, making like wide-eyed tourists. After wandering through a chamber of thrones, choir chairs, and paintings, then into a vaulted apse-shaped chapel with stained glass windows and a glimmering golden altar, they stood atop the dark, tight wooden stairway to the crypt. Simonetta touched a finger to her lips. She unlatched the rope barrier and they stepped in. She re-latched it and they minced down, hands brushing both walls.

The place smelled of old moist bricks, sour, with a vestige of spent candles. They both noted that faded wet footsteps, haphazard spills, and streaks of water went up the stairs. Without mentioning it, they turned right, at the bottom, where a couple of steps descended to the crypt. The water was three or four centimeters below the second step and looked slightly more than ankle deep. "You sure you don't want me to...?" Rich asked. "No, Reech, you're the lookout." She pulled her cap back on. She was quickly out of her shoes and into her high-water boots, which slipped on easily. "Cough if somebody comes," she hushed. "Better yet, sneeze. On second thought...don't do anything."

"Watch your head," he advised, as she stepped with a *plop* into the brown water of the crypt's only obvious chamber. She showed her teeth. "*È ghiacciata*" (It's ice cold). Top-heavy with low vaulted "bat-wing" arches beneath squat columns, the room was the size of an extra-large bedroom; its skin of wall-bricks and bricked-up recesses, centuries-deep, spoke of masons long-vanished in the vacuum of time. Near the back, in the center, sat a stone altar whitened under hidden spotlights.

The chamber was not especially dark in front; still, she shone the powerful flashlight onto every ledge or crevice that might conceal an object the size of a book. Rich chuckled at her serious face and the restless movements of her almond-shaped eyes. *"Accidenti"* (damn), she complained under her breath. She pivoted and scanned the left wall, left to right, up and down. Then, moving farther into the chamber, she directed her beam along the rear wall and under a dark arch past the altar.

Beyond the arch a murky space broke away from the main room and suggested another part of the crypt. "I see something." Her called-out whisper shushed from arch to arch. "Something back there." She steadied the light and looked over her shoulder at Rich. "Can you see? Way in the back there? On a ledge?" He croaked a negative response. She advanced toward the dark rear arch; the slow sloshing of water gave him a sickly feeling that made him think of sewers.

A man's voice: "Who's down there?" She jerked her flashlight; he stiffened, raised a palm. With a *clink*, someone unlatched the barrier cord atop the stairs. Seconds of silence. Rich felt the person thinking. More silence. Footsteps faded. The crypt was open for business. He nodded and mouthed *va bene.*

She reached the dark arch and tripped on a submerged step. Rich lurched in sympathetic reaction. Continuing on, she all but disappeared from his view, leaving only her right elbow silhouetted.

She's got spunk.

He heard a sharp metallic squeak and then another; something opening and closing. A moment later she headed back; she aimed the flashlight at a dark gray box, which she cradled in front of her on her forearm. It was the about size of a hefty box of chocolates. It bore a label; she read it in a deliberately awed voice: "Leonardo Tron, the Secret Work." He nodded vigorously but she shook her head and opened the chillingly squeaky lid. The box was empty. He shrugged, turned up vacant palms.

She switched off her light and sloshed toward the front of the crypt—then stopped cold as if an unseen power seized her.

"*Cosa?*" (What?) Rich asked.

She looked to her left, to the side of the ancient altar, and turned on her light. He saw her mouth open wide like a rattlesnake's, the box and flashlight hit the water as her whole body recoiled. "Simonetta! What? What? What?" His feet smacked the icy water and kicked open the putrid sound of it. He clutched her, following her stare along the bobbing beam of light. A man, dolphin-like, lay on his side half behind the altar, face half submerged. "Blood!" Simonetta sputtered, trembling. "We're in his blood!" She splashed toward the entrance as Rich snatched the box and flashlight from the water. He noted a squirmy pool of red-brown oil around the big bald head and the severed, gaping neck. His wet fingers tingled with the filthy horror.

They crouched near the bottom of the stairs, huddling; his hand cupped the top her cap. "I'm okay," she said in a stifled voice, still shaking. Their lips were not far apart; and he felt the magnetic draw of his to hers along with a flashed mansion-image recalling Jefferson's D.C. memorial. He felt if he kissed her death would disappear, cease to be a problem. Ethereal organ music spread out above them as if to provide a service for the deceased. "I'm okay," she repeated, and they loosened their embrace. She looked up the stairs. "Now...we have to...somehow..." Rich completed her sentence in English: *"Get our asses out of here."*

***

Having merged with a tourist group, Rich and Simonetta wandered out of the church; they hastened along the *riva* to Leo's house a short jog away. Without pause, Leo dutifully called the police to report the body "found by my niece, who was taking photos in the crypt, and who came to me immediately, nearly speechless, poor thing." He thought it wise to leave out Rich completely; he was a foreigner and his presence could lead to complications. Later a *commissario*, a friend of Leo, and two other agents questioned her. It was only she who was in the crypt; she was there to take a photo for her little newspaper; no one was around; she had forgotten her cell phone.

The adjustment and suppression of facts did not trouble Leo, because the alternative was out of the question. An account of his caper would have been bad enough; but the addition of the weird coincidences, which left even him shaking his head, would have been too much: those involving the name *Tron;* the plum pudding story; a stalking lady with a book by Carl Jung, and her tussle with an equally mysterious, bald-headed Asian man—who so happened to look like the dead man—would have built up a mad-house of "clues" before the dead-panned faces of the police.

Over several tables throughout the afternoon Rich and Simonetta tossed around half-digested experiences, further detailing for Leo the previous days' events. He said he knew nothing about the boy on the bridge with the flaming baby story; the Tron connection must have been an ordinary coincidence. Simonetta took the gondoletta back home, where she moored it, and then she and Rich returned to Leo's on foot, flamingo-pink clouds behind them in the western sky and before them in the medley of city windows. Seated with them around the dining table were Oscar Fantini, the actor who in fact played the old man on the roof, and Alberto Cecchino, a clean-shaven, florid-faced man about Leo's age who played Doge Tradonico on Simonetta's phone.

Leo stoked the flames in his imposing fireplace.

"Assuming, Rich, that the dead man was the same you saw fighting with the woman, this alone would make you a material witness."

"I'm not sure it was him," Rich submitted, swirling his cognac. "I couldn't say yes or no about him."

"I'm glad to hear that." He sat down.

"But I have to say—"

"The important thing is we reported the body."

"—it probably was him."

"I admit it's peculiar that a man who looked like him rang your bell and asked for Leonardo Tron."

"It was a man's voice," Rich explained. "So I assume—"

Simonetta cut in: "You think that woman killed him with her umbrella? Maybe it's got a blade in it or something."

Rich shrugged. "Sounds like Hollywood. It's always the same, however, the coincidence-thing. It's like a house of mirrors. Even the old 'Jung-man,' the 'plum-pudding hobo' or whatever you want to call him, whom I remember from whenever; he looked liked Oscar here—I mean the character Oscar so convincingly played that night on the roof. Are you sure it wasn't you that day with the old suitcase?"

Oscar cackled. "Wasn't me. Unless I was drunk."

Rich shook his head and puffed.

"It was enough to freeze my ass off out there on the roof waiting for you to turn the light on."

"And now the book is gone," Simonetta said. "What about that? Somebody killed the man over the book!"

Leo grunted and waved a hand. "Leave all that alone. Somebody took the book. Leave it at that."

"And cut his throat," Simonetta rejoined.

"I'll find out about the dead man. I'll have my people ask at the church about the book. It may even be under water."

"It's in the murderer's pocket."

Leo tossed up his hands as if to throw paltry bits of paper to the wind. He gave a long, reflective sigh and shook his head. "Whatever the case...I've lost my touch, haven't I?"

Simonetta pouted in protest, "No you haven't."

"My comparatively easy scenario did not come off. A man is dead. Mind if an old has-been smokes a cigar to comfort himself?"

Simonetta tisked at his self-deprecation.

He snipped the end off a long Cuban. "What's the English expression, Rich? *'Too much time in my hands'?"*

Rich forced a throaty chuckle. *"On my hands."*

Alberto spoke up: "So this scenario of yours, the book in particular..." He poured himself more cognac. "I must admit I never caught on to it."

Rich nodded. "Yes, Leo, what is it about exactly? It's not a valuable piece, is it?"

Leo blew smoke into the sparkling chandelier. "Well"—he cocked his head and laughed—"from what I've heard today, I'm beginning to think it was more valuable than I realized."

"Yes," Simonetta agreed.

He examined his cigar. "You see, for one thing, I thought Rich would like to translate it into English, rediscover it, you might say. It probably fits into some offbeat historical niche. I'm sure it must. Sixteenth-century it is. Far as I can tell, however, no one, or very few people, has ever heard of Leonardo Tron. That's the name on the cover. The title is interesting enough: *I radici viventi della possibilità" (The Living Roots of Possibility)*. No publisher is noted on the volume. At one time I checked the Biblioteca Marciana, the Archivo di Stato, asked around. "It's in the Tuscan vernacular, not the Venetian. An odd work. I mean it's odd in the way old mystical writings can be."

"A bit of Western esotericism, sounds like," Rich said. "I'm thinking of Agrippa von Nettesheim's *De occulta philosophia* which native son Casanova used to play around with—and dupe people with."

"The title is familiar. Yes, that's probably the category. But even stuff written in the twentieth century. I have a quirky book from around 1910 in which the author tells the reader to drink rainwater during a thunderstorm to get"—he wiggled his fingers—"'magnetic power.' I found the Tron book amusing, funny, in the same way. I remember... What was it now? Yes, there was something...something about *blinking*, blinking one's eyes to make things happen."

He stood up, cleared his throat. "I read it a few years ago, part of it." He padded over to the fireplace. "It had to do with..." He leaned on a fancy carved pillar and looked into the restless flames. "Its main subject..." He narrowed his eyes and then looked up at everyone. "It has to do with controlling possibilities, things that might happen but didn't yet happen. That's it. Possibilities, as in the title. Stopping bad possibilities. Matter of fact, there's a whole practice to it. Well, sure, its subtitle is *A Practical Discourse*. It was meant to be *used,* this book. It's been sitting like a sore thumb in my family library, along with the five-thousand other volumes, goodness, since before I was born, I would say."

Rich raised his hand, as if back in school. "You said few people have heard of the book or the author." He stretched open his battered pack of cigarettes and made blank face at seeing only one. "There are other people who know about it?"

Leo ambled over to the windows and leaned back against a long ledge-like chest. He puffed his cigar. "A couple of summers ago I received a visit from a man who heard from a former assistant of mine that I owned this book. A tall, skinny guy, he was, a string bean in a white linen suit. What was his name now? English, I think. Worthington? Extremely articulate gentleman. The book I had was the first part of a two-volume work. I knew there was more than one volume, because mine, in fact, had *Divided into Two Books* on the title page. He had searched for years thinking it was a single book. Then, somewhere in the Middle East, no, North Africa, I believe, he located a person who had the second volume. Fèz, Morocco, that's where it was. The owner let him read it, on condition that he not copy it or remove it from his personal library. Now something happened, I forget what. Whatever it was it prevented him from reading far into the book. I recall he was distraught over having to abandon it. A revolt. A fire. I don't remember. He was forced to leave the country. I never give away or sell my books, but I let him copy mine. He photographed it right here with one of those thin little spy cameras, which I thought rather quaint—and funny, considering it was about as skinny he was. He was extremely grateful and sent me a case of fine Scotch as a gift. He came off, at first, as a collector, not a scholar. But the text obviously interested him more. About a year ago, I remember now, I received an email from him to the effect that I should hide the book, keep quiet about it, something. I didn't pay attention to it; he had an eccentric streak, you know. I forgot about it until the other day."

Rich made a pained face. "I'm sorry the book is gone. It's really sparked my interest now. You know, if you wanted me to translate it you could have easily handed it to me."

With an enigmatic, beard-stretching smile, Leo came as close to blushing as Rich ever thought possible. Gazing down, he moved from the windows and crept around the table. Simonetta made a soft sound of agreement; she stroked Rich's thigh, making his nose twitch.

Right here in public.

"Well," Leo said, "the old passion is still in the veins. As soon as I heard where you lived, in Corte Tron, I made the distant connection and it all came together in my head." He chuckled. "What can I say, Rich? Welcome to the family!"

Everyone laughed.

"Thank you. I think."

"I yearn for it, you know. The whole scenario came to me in an instant, everything." He snapped his fingers. "I suppose it's like writing fiction with reality. My art. Well, maybe you got to know...had a little fun together. I hope so..."

Rich and Simonetta's wry sighs collided.

"...despite..."

"I know I certainly did," Alberto put in.

Rich scratched his temple, closed one eye. "Well, yes. We did too."

"I must say, Uncle Leo, the crypt was a bit much."

He lowered his head and nodded. "Yes, a little wet."

"Among other things," she added darkly.

"We had to solve a few transmission problems down there." He looked thoughtfully to one side. "You know, when I said that, a minute ago, about Corte Tron, where you live, I remembered another thing about the book. We skip the most obvious things. It did, of course, have to do with coincidences. Preventing coincidences, was it? The absence of thought, the cancellation of thoughts, thinking and not thinking. Blinking thoughts away." He huffed. "I'd like to blink off a few thoughts now and then." With a serious brow, he looked down and puffed his cigar.

Voiceless relaxation set in, signaling the end of the evening. Leo became withdrawn. Rich wondered if he was reassessing his attitude toward the book and feeling remorse over having treated the volume lightly. No one seemed willing to plot a further "story" for the mysterious events except Simonetta. "So...our next move..." she quietly contemplated.

She stayed at the house and Leo asked Gigio Mattone, the "bouncer-type" Rich had spoken to at the carnival party, to take Rich home in the motor launch.

They cruised the Grand Canal. Again muscle-bound Gigio surprised him with his learned comments. He pointed out the hotel where Ruskin stayed; the Casetta Rossa where super-wordsmith D'Annunzio resided while planning his wartime exploits; Palazzo Barbaro, which Henry James used in *Wings of the Dove;* Ca' Rezzonico, where Robert Browning had lived; Palazzo Giustinian, where Wagner wrote the second act of *Tristan and Isolde;* Palazzo Balbi, from which Napoleon (*"Quel piccolo stronzo"* — that little turd) viewed a regatta in his honor.

The canal was all night-lighted; and with its shimmering fish-bone-like reflections, it was even more magical, uncanny, than in the daytime, because of one "peculiar" fact: The "Patriarch of Streams" succumbed to the inevitability of night same as all the common waterways and main streets of the world. As often happened, he wished his mother were there to see it.

An hour later, with a scratchy throat, two aspirin in him, and a bag of popcorn, he sat in darkness warm and bundled up in bed watching with half-closed eyes the 1939 movie *Andy Hardy Gets Spring Fever* on his laptop. It was soothing to be in the small town of Carvel with young Mickey Rooney, who fell for his teacher, and Lewis Stone, who played his wise and understanding father, Judge Hardy, who grew woolly jowls, as around his floating bench in his dark, stinking court he judged a hundred naked, weeping souls; pounding his spiked gavel, wrapping his tail around himself, his eyes wheels of flame. "Aw!" Rich closed his laptop, Dante's scrambled inferno fading. "Go to hell!" He eased into a pleasanter repose, but not before saying the word *heaven*, as he thought *hell* should not be the last word spoken before falling asleep.

***

On the night of Rich's dark little half-dream, Simonetta was wide awake at Leo's. She was composing a classified ad she hoped would call forth more information about the Tron mystery.

At the same time, on the other side of town, Ornella Riusi, the seventeen-year-old girl who claimed she saw a horrible beast atop her neighborhood arch, stood naked before a dozen breadsticks neatly lined up like prison bars on her sister's kitchen table. She closed her eyes for a moment, then reopened them and stared at the sticks. She left the darkened kitchen for the living room, where all the lights were on and the shutters open. She closed her eyes again and stood still for several minutes. She sighed with frustration, ran her fingers through her black-rooted blond hair and then went to the front door. She unlocked it and opened it wide. The air in the stairway felt unpleasantly cool on her winter-white body.

She stepped out onto the landing, where she paused. She started down the stairs, eyes closed, fingers brushing the thick wooden railing. The air and the hard floor beneath her bare feet became colder as she descended. A TV or radio program played gently in a second-floor apartment. When she reached the ground level she opened her eyes and pushed open the big door to the street. The frigid breath of the night bit into her frontally.

She stepped out into the dark, deserted calle, the pavement like ice beneath her feet. Rippling with chills, she looked at the slender brick arch at the end of her lane and closed her eyes. Arms at her side, feet together, she stood still—or tried to.

"No!" She shattered her stance and dashed back inside, thoughtlessly slamming the front door. She quickly and lightly scaled the stairs—just out of sight of a neighbor, who opened his door and saw one bare foot vanish atop the flight above.

Her teeth chattering, her body cascading with shivers, she stood by the stove. It was still warm from her dinner. She studied the breadsticks and spoke to steady herself: "I slammed the door. I wasn't *thinking* when I slammed the door. I didn't care. That was good, but..." She leaned forward on the table and examined the sticks. "They're still only bread."

She sighed. "I'm sorry, signor Tron."

Chapter Two

Great! A perfect night's sleep, practically dreamless; and what dreams there hadn't been sparkled now in waking flecks touched with the kiss of long-lost carefree eras and joy-spells.

Gosh, I feel good this morning!

Rich had always wondered whether other people had flecks. When a person is exuberant (he put to an imaginary audience), is there not an atomic level of kindred imagery, of stored experience that springs forth in charged kindred memory-bits, even if one is barely conscious of it? Someday, he thought, he would do a book about flecks, which included his poems and a technical discourse.

Anyway, the "Tron Affair" is over. Maybe I can get my mind back, think about really important things. Like flecks.

But a wiser part of him suspected the "Tron Affair" was not over; and the rest of him, which had happily splashed around under the wiser part's courteously concealed eye, was convinced of it when Simonetta called and told him about the ad she wrote for the classifieds page of a local newspaper.

"Listen to this, Reech: 'Researcher is interested in hearing from anyone who recently experienced anything unusual in connection with the surname Tron.' Then I give my phone number."

"Are you sure you want to do this?"

"I did it. I called it in five minutes ago."

He discharged a long, hollow groan that reminded him of the sound a large sleeping dog makes when having a nightmare.

She laughed. "What was *that!*"

He snorted a chuckle, having surprised himself with his lugubrious canine eruption. "I don't know," he sulked.

"I was going to mention the missing book but I think that would have been too much. I think we shouldn't mention the book, or books, to anyone. Keep that part quiet."

"Yes. Keep it quiet. I'm not really sure what we're after, Simonetta. Are we looking for trouble?"

"Ah, dearest tesorino, I'm glad you said *we.* No, I have this feeling that more is going to come out of this. Something is happening, no? A man is dead; people looking for, fighting over, Leonardo Tron. Something is going on nobody knows about."

"Well," he said, "sounds like trouble."

"There's nothing in the paper about the dead man. Seems pretty hush-hush. Murder in Venice is a big deal, you know. It hardly ever happens. Uncle Leo's waiting to hear more."

A minute later they hung up, promising to keep each other up to date on developments. He put down his phone and contrived another drawn-out dog sound, attempting to recreate and study the involuntary one, but without success. Before long he would have the opportunity to produce yet another expression of animal agony—after a knock on his door.

He ate a *panino di tonno* (tuna sandwich) at lunchtime on the foggy Rialto and returned home with a loaf of bread and a new pack of American cigarettes. The dull weather had snuffed his expansive morning exuberance and shackled his spirits to a stubborn present. Simonetta's phone call had prefaced the bondage. He got comfy on the sofa with an anthology of Leopardi's poems. The poet's sweetly rendered but crushing loneliness was a bad choice, and he returned the book to its proper pile. Audible thoughts invaded; namely, the *thump-thump-thumping* of the recorded pop music that had so annoyed him in the Rialto snack bar. On top of the thumping, his dwindling financial condition raided his mind and he imagined himself with his bags packed, standing on an airstrip waiting to board a silver 1940s aircraft. He snickered at this image, which he realized was a carryover from his beloved classic movies.

He took out his Smartphone to read the news. When away from the U.S., he rarely kept track of current events. He relished this serene detachment from the ordinary markings of time. Now he saw by accident a headline in *Il Gazzettino*. *"Rimasta vedova del gatto, ora Dominique vuole sposare il suo cane."*("Widowed by her cat, now Dominique wants to marry her dog.")

Okay, enough of this!

Then there was the knock on the door. It jolted him through and through.

Who the hell?

He bolted up and propelled himself toward the door. Without further consideration he pulled it open.

As a cartoon character's face retains the shape of the frying pan that struck it, so did Rich's emotional state feel imprinted with the doorway sight and everything it embraced: It was the mysterious trench-coated woman who had followed him two days before, the woman with the Jung book, the woman who beat with her umbrella the pudgy Asian man who later wound up —

"Buon giorno," she asserted.

"Buon giorno," he replied, restraining a howl he thought would have frightened Cerberus the three-headed hell-dog.

Her perfume smelled like pine-scented turpentine.

Simonetta, I have to tell you what happened.

"In che posso servirLa" (How can I help you)?

"Sorry, I don't speak Italian, only read it." She had an unusual British-like accent he was unable to place.

"That's all quite right. Quite all right."

"Professor Travella, I presume?"

"Well, associate professor. Now I'm not that either, I presume." He managed a chuckle and rocked his head.

"Very sorry to bother you. My name is Emma Mead. They gave me your name and address at the university."

Bastards. Haven't I got a phone?

"I thought perhaps you could lead me in the right direction concerning some research I'm involved in."

"We shall see, we shall see."

Why do I suddenly feel British?

He invited her in with a hand sweep. He had not realized how good-looking she was. *Emma Mead?* Why, she reminded him of the actress Mary Astor but with the sleeker elongations of Hedy Lamarr. He thought she bore a slight Celtic impishness sometimes visible in work of the Pre-Raphaelite painters. She was about thirty-five. Only one small particular marred her good looks: a morsel of snot nestled at the rim of her left nostril.

"Have a seat." He was tempted to point out the package of tissues on the end table near her chair.

"Chilly outside," she noted, sitting down.

"Yes, a chilly day. A trifle gloomy."

He marveled at how he boxed up his nervousness.

"So nice and warm in here."

Maybe I'm not really nervous.

He thought she looked slick with that tilted black beret atop her shiny jet-black permanent-waved hair, direct from film noir. When she opened her glossy new raincoat she revealed a black leather turtleneck over tight black and gray leopard-print pants.

But that pistachio crumb in her nose!

Rather than pace in his edgy "classroom" fashion, he sat on the sofa facing her across the rectangular glass coffee table.

Remember, this is a fact-finding enterprise.

"So, you're doing research?"

"Yes, I'd like to know —"

He offered her his pack of cigarettes.

"Oh, thank you."

I knew the dame smoked.

He sensed a shift in his personality from Brit to Bogart. He took a cigarette for himself and lit hers first. Sitting back, he saw the face of detective Sam Spade visit his own face.

Damn booger is ruining the scene, though.

He resisted the impulse to rest his feet on the table and cross his ankles in Bogey fashion.

I should have burned it out.

She blew smoke to one side. "I was wondering if you've ever heard of a certain work, a book."

Okay, get ready.

"I believe it's titled—excuse my pronunciation—*I radici viventi della possibilità.*" She flicked a negligible ash. "It's by a sixteenth-century author named Leonardo Tron."

Okay, she's not a murderess.

"The Living Roots of Possibility," he translated, with a show of fascination.

But suppose she does have the book and is after the second volume? Great question!

"H'mmm..." He tipped back his imaginary fedora. "Catchy title. I don't think I've heard of it. Is it a one-volume work?"

"Yes, I believe so."

She's got a lot to learn.

"Tron, of course, is a historical Venetian family name, a patrician name. I live in Corte Tron, right here, as you know."

"Yes, that's a bit of a...something or other."

She's afraid of the word coincidence.

"What sort of book is it?"

"Well, it's a mystical work of a kind, so I hear, but with scientific, real-world applications, it is said."

"Of course, that's typical of lot of mystics, you know — alchemists, protoscience types, so forth."

"Yes, of course, you're right about that."

"People could get into trouble for that sort of thing. How did you find out about this book? What makes it special?"

"Well, it's... I have an interest in the subject. I'm doing some writing and...I've heard here and there in my research esoteric things about the book I thought I could use."

"I see."

Let's pour it on a bit.

He made a steeple of his fingertips and looked at the ceiling with a strained face. "Would this *mirabilis liber*...relate to post-Reformation visionaries and reformers? You know, utopian thought more or less contemporaneous with the fresh exegesis of canon at Trent. There was the inevitable conflict, of course, between exegesis and eisegesis, in which I would not include that fascination of theirs with church and state in the Venetian Republic. They were all over Venice at the time, in fact, lecturing from rooftops, having audiences, getting into mischief. I'm thinking along the lines of Dionisio Gallo, whom Doctor Marion Leathers Kuntz so capably researched. Might it be in that category?"

She sprayed smoke and licked her lips. "I, well, it's—"

"Ha!" He slapped his knee. "Forgive me, I always think of that salutation of his in a *Legatio* to the Venetian Senate. I memorized it for fun. Get this: *'Ad illustrissimum, grausissimum, aequissimum et potentissimum Dominium vniuersumque clarissimum, Senatum Venetum.'* Talk about blowing smoke!"

"Um, yes, indeed, that's *something*. You know, there are certain discrepancies—descriptions, I mean—of magic in it, I gather, but it's supposed to be more psychological and in a scientific way. It involves thought, doing things with thought."

"Oh, you mean like"—he pulled a random name from Italian literature, contextually irrelevant and fictitiously adorned—"Luigi Pulci, who went before the *Consiglio dei Dieci?*"

"Yes, I gather it's sort of like that."

"Lucky for him he was judged *non malus, sed amens.*"

"Yes, lucky!" She leaned forward and pounded out her butt. Then, as she looked up, a cold blade sliced the niceness. It shivered through him. They locked looks, voices stuck. He saw evil prick the corner of her eye, felt his heart beat faster.

She knows I know about the book and that she knows I know she knows.

The evil dissolved as quickly as it came.

"Well," she aspirated, grasping with a slap her leopard-print knees, "I ask you only to keep an eye out for it, perhaps inquire around if you get a chance." They both stood up.

"I will. I'll let you know. Do you have — ?"

"I'll give you my card." She took one from her pocket. "Just my email address. I travel a lot."

As he looked at the self-printed card he noted she gave the room behind him the once-over, her eyes a nervous bird's. He boldly looked up and caught her searching. "Okay, thanks."

Frowning, she mouthed a "thank you" and swallowed. He wondered, was it disappointment or suppressed anger?

In the few seconds of painful silence as they stepped toward the door, unresolved questions flooded his mind.

Should Bogey rip off the cap and gown and stop pussyfooting?

She paused at the door. Emotionless, she faced him, moved in close, hands in her pockets. Then, evenly, in a low, serious voice: "Finding it for me would be very much worth your while."

He made a wiry inquisitive sound.

Boy, what a lame squeak.

She moved a step closer, much too close now. "How about we say...to the tune of one hundred thousand U.S. dollars?"

Twice overcome, he nevertheless made one of the socially boldest moves he had ever dared. "Hold still, sister." In a single smooth movement he reached to one side, whisked a tissue from the package on the table and clutched her nose with it. Pulling off, he captured the undisciplined particle.

You're beautiful again, sweetheart.

She stared at him with stunned eyes. "Oh," she gasped, her expression unchanged, "thank you."

"Don't mention it."

He let her out and thought of adding, *tell Carl Jung I said hello.* Returning to himself, he pressed his back against the closed door.

Omigod... Omigod...

He tossed his tissue-wrapped trophy into a basket.

***

Windy, cold but partly sunny, with choppy water — this was the atmosphere of the following afternoon; and Simonetta, in the vaporetto boat with Rich, was all this in herself — choppy and breezy with excitement — all except cold and partly anything. She was an animated flame, a rosy-cheeked beam, still on her toes from Rich's account of his meeting with so-called Emma Mead and from the response she had gotten from her newspaper ad.

"You're not *bipolare*, are you?" Rich asked.

"Probably! *E non me ne frega!*" (And I don't give a damn!)

The water-bus plowed south on the Grand Canal toward the San Tomà stop, which station is right before the great *volta* or curve that carves out the north side of Dorsoduro. The stop is a short walk to the Gran Scuola di San Rocco, the sixteenth-century confraternity building, in front of which Ornella Riusi had asked Simonetta to meet her at one o'clock. She promised to explain where she fit into the Tron mysteries and tell all about *"il Grande Tron,"* who she claimed she had met this very morning. She said he taught her great things, which he read in "funny Italian" from a "pretty purple notebook with pink glitter all over it." Simonetta was surprised that Ornella was accustomed to the name Tron as a person rather than only as a street near her home. It was Simonetta who had used the name *Leonardo* first, but soon the girl began to talk about him using his name as if she knew him.

"I'm looking forward to this!" she told Rich before boarding the vaporetto. It'll be a good diversion."

"Diversion?"

"I mean, at first I thought she was talking about some local guy she knew. She seemed *fine* through all that, if a little childish in a sing-song kind of way. I mean she seemed okay up to the point when I asked her if she understood that the person I was referring to lived five-hundred years ago."

Rich felt the straight-man imperative: "Then what did she say?"

"She said, 'Yes, I know. That's him!'"

Simonetta shot a sharp laugh, which despite the roar of the motor turned the heads of passengers. Rich staged a wary face. Seeing his reaction, she said, "Well, Reech, I think we should cover every aspect, don't you?"

He nodded crookedly. "Well, it'll be fun."

"That's the spirit!" She slapped him on the back.

They disembarked at San Tomà. Simonetta knew the way and walked with her usual sprightly pace. Rich had visited the Scuola di San Rocco several times, to take in the Tintorettos (the institution is said to be the painter's "Sistine Chapel"), but had never approached it from the San Tomà area. He liked the fresh unfamiliarity of the neighborhood's intimate *calli* and *campi* and without speaking began to lead the way excitedly.

"Where are we going?" She squealed. "What's come over you?"

"I'm getting 'elsewhere-everywhere' feelings, near and far. Turn here!" She went along with his fine frenzy, accepting his blind, exhilarated logic. "I feel the mansion, the castle, creating itself. Turn here! I knew these streets a thousand years ago. The countless rooms. I'll know them a thousand hence! This way!" They went through a dark sotopòrtego and onto the Fondamenta di Donna Onesta, where they crossed a narrow canal.

"I need to find a corner to press myself into, Simonetta, near a window, and from that window see other sunlit angles, bridges, white minarets hushed blue from the unseen ocean, which might take me to other elsewheres, like Marco Polo. That way!"

"What are you *talking* about!"

"You've read my poems! Then there are the high windows you can't see out of, like when I was a kid and would bring home empty refrigerator boxes and cut a single square near the top. I'd sit on the bottom so I couldn't see out and then look at how the light touched the walls of the box. All the flecks of times and places. Who knew what worlds lay beyond the box! This way!"

"No!" Simonetta commanded. "This way!"

He huffed to a stop. "Sorry. It was my turn. One of my poetic frenzies. Or maybe a musical frenzy. Oh, the same thing."

"You're not *autistico*, are you?"

"I don't know. *E non me ne frega!*"

Holding hands they hurried over the small Ponte San Rocco, re-crossing the canal, and into the Campiello San Rocco. "Oh, wait! I know where we are!" Through the Sotopòrtego San Rocco he saw familiar clouds of dark green foliage against the red brick gothic back of Santa Maria Gloriosa dei Frari, one of the city's most important basilicas for art and tomb-work. "I love it when that happens. When you don't know where you are, then suddenly you know, but from a new angle."

"That seems to be your great joy in life."

"Well, something like that. It's all related. Hey, you know, the tomb of Niccolò Tron is in the Frari."

They emerged in Campo San Rocco. To their left sat the Church of San Rocco with its smart white façade of Istrian stone and niche'd figures of saints; and to the left of the church, nearly shouldered with it at right angles, the eclectic, ironic pomposity of the confraternal Scuola di San Rocco, with its free-standing Corinthian columns, triple-arched Codussian windows, polychromatic inlays and allegorical carvings. They scanned the tourists in front of the building for young Ornella.

"What is she supposed to look like again?" Rich asked.

"She's blondish; said she'd be wearing a brown double-breasted coat and pink and blue knitted beanie. I don't see anybody like that. Let's keep moving; it's getting colder. She'll probably come from over there, beside the church."

Fifteen minutes past the designated time and still no Ornella. The sun went in; and at that moment, Rich, for some reason, caught a charged mental fleck of Nassau Street in Princeton.

"We should have met inside someplace," he said.

"A nice warm bar. Wait a second." She squinted at the people who had halted in the narrow passage between the church and the Scuola. "I think that's her. See the hat?"

"What's she got there? She's stopping people."

"I don't know. Newspaper? Something in newspaper."

Simonetta waved her hand. She got the girl's attention and they approached one other. Now they saw that she had a dozen fresh sardines resting on a wet, dirty-looking bed of newspaper; she held it before her on both palms like a serving tray.

"Ciao, Ornella? I'm Simonetta. This is my friend Reech."

"It's a shame to throw them out," Ornella whined. "You want to take them home? I bought them this morning."

"What are you doing with those, dear?" Rich heard sympathy in her use of the word *dear.*

"Well, I thought if I studied them..." She stared at the fish. She wrinkled her nose and shook her head. "Oh never mind." They cringed when the girl, after a slight hesitation, rolled up the sardines and stuffed the package into a pocket of her fat-buttoned brown coat. "So, you know, I really think, on the arch, what I saw on the arch, the creature, was, you know... I really think it was the Lion of Saint Mark."

"Oh, you think so?" Simonetta asked. "You've come to this conclusion?" She sent a glance to Rich, who sent one back.

"I hope so. The thing is I don't remember seeing any wings. And the lion wasn't peaceful; no, wasn't peaceful. They should have wings, no? Do all the Saint Mark lions have wings?"

Rich searched his mind for a wingless one.

I ought to know that.

He knew that peace was not their primary aspect, despite the *"pax tibi"* inscribed in the Gospel volume that they rest a paw on. The Republic of Venice, Saint Mark's word, elevated spirituality, Christ Triumphant... The symbols went on and on.

Simonetta spoke up. "It's cold out. What do you say we—?"

"That lion really roared, too, scared me really bad! My mask fell off. I stepped on it."

A roaring lion... Paganism untamed?

"I peed in my nice gown."

"Ornella, Reech, let's find a restaurant, a place to sit."

Saint Jerome had a sweet pet lion.

"Reech?"

"Huh? Oh, good idea!"

The Lion of Juda.

"But we have to go in here first," Ornella asserted.

"Oh, you want to go into the Scuola?"

"That's why we're meeting here. Signor Tron told me about the pictures and about his book. You said you were interested."

"Yes, yes, we want you to—" Her serious face took a step back, disarmed by the word *book,* as she had never brought up the book in their phone chat. She glanced at Rich and they exchanged silent gasps.

"Oh, the book, yes, how did you—? Do you mean the pretty purple notebook he read from?"

"No, not that. Some other book, an old, old book. But I don't think he meant the lion's holy book. He meant another one, the missing book. Are we going inside?"

Rich and Simonetta elbowed one another and followed her.

As they passed through the portal of the Scuola the symbolism of Ornella's beast-vision would not leave Rich alone; and he plucked from somewhere in the Bible, *Be sober, be vigilant; because your adversary the devil, as a roaring lion, walketh about, seeking whom he may devour.* His face beat hotly. He shook off the sensation and sketched out a speedy sign of the cross.

Simonetta paid the admission and in a moment they stood in the brown dusk of the huge *salone terreno,* a colonnaded, marbled-floored "warehouse" whose walls were spaced with arched curtained windows and Tintoretto's earth-warm panels of the life of the Virgin and the infant Christ; canvases pensively rendered in varying grades of finish, a "poverty" of brushwork said to deliberately offset the charitable foundation's opulence. Curiously, the place smelled faintly of fresh oil paint.

"All the way in back," Ornella said, swinging her finger right and left. "They're on both sides of the altar." A whiff of sardines made Rich want to inject a "something's fishy" jest, but he knew it would not intelligibly translate into Italian.

They neared the white marble altar, to the left. Behind and above it a soaring temple-like background enshrined a statue of anti-plague Saint Rocco. Ornella pointed to a painting on the left wall. In the lower right of an umber-dark, selectively luminous landscape, a haloed woman comfortably sat, casually reading a book. She wore a gold-belted red robe and an amply pooled brown cloak. The restless rendering of foliage and shrubbery, a tortured anthropomorphic tree, and a sky caught between night and day haunted the mystic scene.

"Look at her," Ornella hushed with wonderment.

"Mary Magdalene," Rich commented, recalling the image.

She shook a "no-no" finger, which he thought was meant to cast the first stone at Mary. "That's who they *say* she is."

"Right, there's debate about that." Rich wondered how she knew.

"Over here now." She pivoted and rushed over to the wall on the other side where a companion painting hung.

"Now look at *her*."

"It's the same person, but viewed from the back, probably even the same landscape, in the opposite direction."

"Yes, it is," Simonetta agreed.

Ornella held up a finger and smiled craftily, showing a row of tiny teeth. "But they say she's Saint Mary of Egypt. Why?"

He nearly came out with "Mary, Mary, quite contrary," but again kept in check his comedic instinct, this time because he sensed the girl was moving toward a real esoteric reading that was not very well known. He recalled that the two figures represented the "World Mother" in a certain theological interpretation.

"And she looks up from the book now. It's what she's doing—*not doing*, I mean, here. That's important."

"Go on," he prompted. This point was new to him.

She looked down, pulled in her lips and wrinkled her narrow, slightly needled nose; she made as if to hold a head-sized sphere, which she gently tilted right, then left. "It's the *on* and the *off,*" she affirmed melodiously, and as she said it she wiggled her behind left to right. "It's the power that's there when the brain's not there, not there. Tron said this was my big problem. I might have too much brain. The book she's reading. That's thinking. When she's not reading the book, that's forgetting the book, what's in the book. The *on* and the *off.*" Again she did her little derrière dance and paused. "Well, maybe I got it backwards. Anyway, she's not, not doing, not thinking, he told me. It's nothing. Well, not nothing. Something happens. That's when it happens. Yes, that's what he said. The front picture is our front and the back is our back. That's it. Miracles happen behind our back. You can't think about it — them. If you think about them you stop the... Well, you zap it."

"Zap it," Rich repeated.

"The innocence!"

"Okay."

The girl's words continued to beguile him, because even the secondary, philosophic part of her lecture contained an echo of something he had recently heard, from a wholly different source.

Thinking. Not thinking. What Leo said. Something in the Tron book. Cancellation of thought.

"The soul is about brain-thoughts and emotion-motion too — emotion-motion." She made several jerky movements, punching the air in the manner of the 1960s Twist dance. "He said it's male and female, together. Thinking can sometimes smooth out the heart—you know, mistakes, feeling-mistakes; but the Mother Soul has to rescue the brain, rescue your thinking, I mean, from being selfish and all that, with its divine enchantment spirit."

"Okay, so what about Tron and his book?" Simonetta queried. "Is that supposed to be his book in the paintings?"

"Wait. So we've got Joseph and Mary, no? Man, woman? Okay, back to the pictures, the paintings, the one in front of us especially, what I said about not thinking. When she's looking up from reading, up from the words in the book, we see her back, the back of it. That's the Child Mind, the Jesus Mind." She wiggled again. "The Child Mind, the Jesus Mind."

"Right," Rich agreed, "I see your point."

Simonetta added, "Yes, the childlike innocence, the openness. So, what about—"

"I'm glad you both understand. It's really why I have the sardines." She reached down to pull them from her pocket, but four more hands pushed them back.

"A fisher of men... We get it," Rich insisted.

"No," Ornella replied, her voice wilting.

Simonetta rushed in. "Ornella, who is this person Tron you said told you all this?"

"He visited me to ask me if I had a book. He spoke funny Italian; a funny voice he had. I understood, but... He said he asked people about me because he read in the newspaper about seeing me, I mean, me seeing the lion there on the arch."

"What was this person like? Can you describe him?"

"Oh yeah, that's funny. Well, no, over here first." She pointed across the room. "Let's go over here and I'll show you. Follow me." She led the way. "He looks like this sometimes."

Rich and Simonetta traded blank stares as they marched behind her to the front of the long room.

"At first he scared me. That's funny. But look at this."

The girl stopped before the second huge canvas on the left wall not far from the entrance. She pointed to a figure in the *Adoration of the Magi*. Another dark but partially glowing scene, it depicted the holy figures of mother and child, the hovering attendant angels, and the three richly clothed Magi all in luminous contrast with the dilapidated hovel of a manger.

"That's him there." She was pointing to the kneeling pilgrim, who gazed in reverent awe at the miraculous infant.

"I'm right," Rich said to himself in English. Simonetta looked at him questioningly and he switched back to Italian. "I'll tell you later." He was now certain where Ornella's discourse had come from. In fact, he detected a mixture of two, possibly three, separate influences, each an answer but still a puzzlement considering it came from this oddly adjusted girl.

Simonetta turned to Ornella and stroked her shoulder. "Oh, so he actually looks like that? Long beard and all? Bald head? About seventy years old?"

"Well, no, he was furry all around and not bald, I mean when he has his hair on, he said. He likes to dress up in different... different..."

"Disguises?" Simonetta suggested.

Yes, that's it. Disguises. But he's younger, a little more than that man. That's him, but his head-hair is cut. You can see that's him under the fur."

Rich's gaze remained on the kneeling man. The lovingly executed face, aside from providing him with clues, had diverted his thoughts even more, and he felt tears well up in his eyes.

Simonetta saw his change in demeanor and gave a quiet gasp. "What is it, Reech?" Ornella noticed his wet eyes too and gave a long, sympathetic *awww*. She threw herself against him and hugged him. He cupped the top of her crocheted beanie with his hand. Simonetta stepped back with a look of *hey, let me in on this.*

Rich detached the girl. "No, it's...it's the genius of Tintoretto. I never fully... The expression on that man. The awe, the wonderment, no, even more...the pure, intent, selfless, childlike absorption, the quiet hope, humanity, everything... It's just..." He sniffed, lifted his glasses and wiped a tear.

Fixed on Rich, Simonetta, taking her turn, crinkled her face, covered her eyes; sobbing she thrust her head into his chest. Again Ornella followed magnet-like. Three boxers in a clinch. "Okay, okay, let's take it easy. There are all kinds of things going on at once." He cupped his mouth, thought for a moment. "So, Ornella, the man in the painting doesn't really look like the man who called himself Tron? Or he looks like him sometimes, what?"

"Well, sometimes, he said. But me, I don't look like, like the two Marys who are not Marys but the World Mother."

"Ahhh..." Rich nearly exclaimed.

Again Simonetta looked questioningly at him.

He gently grasped Ornella's shoulder. "And so he told you you're a kind of new Messiah, a Jesus-Woman."

Simonetta's eyes widened.

"Yes, he told me. Well, the female so-and-so one. Like in the pictures. But not the World Mother like that. A small one."

"Reech, what exactly — ?"

"I'll explain later. Why does he think this about you?"

She pulled off her Beanie. "I'm hot. Can we leave here?"

"Hot? Oh sure, let's go. Let's take Simonetta's suggestion and find a restaurant." Rich regretted not being able to go upstairs to the Chapter Room, the magnificent *salone* that gave the Scuola its reputation as Tintoretto's "Sistine Chapel." Ten minutes later they sat at a long wooden table in a Bavarian-looking restaurant a few doors away from the Scuola, waiting for their pizzas to arrive. Ornella sat right under a cuckoo clock.

Thump, thump, thump, thump. Too bad. Nice place otherwise.

"So, you stay at your sister's apartment? Simonetta inquired. "Where are your sister and her husband?"

"They're skiing. They're coming back Sunday night."

"And you're doing okay?"

"Oh yes. I'm okay. I cook and clean. I help the neighbors."

"There are neighbors who know you well?"

"Oh yes. We love one another. Ever since I was a baby." They're really nice people. They give me things."

"That's good to know."

Rich continued his inquiry. "So this fellow who calls himself Tron, he told you you might be a female Jesus?"

"Well, it was after he asked me about his book and all, if I had it and I said no, I told him about these feelings I had for a long time. I feel like somebody special. I mean, not special, just, I don't know, touched I guess it is."

"Touched by God?"

She shrugged shyly. "Well...it's like I need to be doing something different and good, secret things. Then he said he knew who I was and had a way for me maybe to do miracles."

"How so?"

"Well, he said it was all in his book. But he said it was all a kind of a test. He really needed that second piece of the book to...make it right or better or work even. He said he forgot what he wrote, but was trying to remember. It's too bad I never saw it because everybody says I have a great memory."

"Did he have the first book with him?"

"Yes, he showed it to me. Old book. He said he just got it, in the morning, same morning. That book was lost too. It had his name on it. Leonardo Tron. He gave me tips. He said it's from the first book. The tips. I really had to shut off my mind. I had to figure out how to think something without thinking about it—like in the paintings—pictures—paintings. The on and the off. He took me here and showed me them. Oh, 'thinking behind your own back,' that's what he called it. I told you. It's hard. There's a place or something, a spot he said. 'Zone' is what he said. That's right—'Zone.' He said that Adam and Eve didn't know they were naked and when they got corrupted they knew. God asked them, 'Who told you you were naked?'" I remembered that myself. You see, their minds were on it. They lost the miracle-mind and could never get it back. The whole world couldn't. Except some people. Saints. But Tron said I might not be one of those after all. My memory is really good and I think too much for it to work. He said I was not—what did he say?—he said I was not wide enough. Oh, not *broad* enough. I don't know what that means. I'll have to take a cure. Smoke some kind of cigarette or—"

"No no!" Simonetta admonished," don't take anything from him. You have to promise me this. Will you?"

She nodded.

"Did your neighbors meet this man?" Rich asked.

"No, he said it has to all be secret."

Their pizzas arrived and Ornella's eyes lit up. As the waiter set down the plates, she made an announcement: "I've started to walk around totally naked." The young male server spilled half of Rich's spritz. "It's the truth!" Ornella declared, pointing at the glass in reaction to the coincidence of her statement and the spill. "I tried walking on the stairs, you know, in the building. I thought if I forgot I was naked my mind would get pure. See what I mean? Then I could work on the breadsticks."

"Oh...the breadsticks?" Rich asked, and then looked at Simonetta, who bore an expression of pained curiosity.

"I know it's silly. It's my idea also. I didn't want to waste a whole lot of bread, like the sardines we threw out. Did I really put those in my pocket? Why did I do that? I don't know. You know how Jesus changed the loaves into fishes? I thought I should start out small, you know, with breadsticks."

Simonetta asked, "So those sardines...?"

"I bought those, I told you. They were only to think about, you know, before trying it this morning again. But it didn't work. I couldn't get the pure mind. Except for a second. If I could think of what sardines looked like and didn't think of being naked and then... Well, I figured I could turn the breadsticks... Well, they're small and they're thin, you know. *Dio mio, che puzzo!* My pocket really *smells.* Why did I do that?"

Simonetta gently questioned her about the man's behavior. It was clear that aside from having filled her head with strange ideas, he had not taken advantage of her. The only physical contact between them was when he shook her hand.

"Did he say he would come back to see you?"

"Oh yes, today. He said at three-thirty."

Simonetta and Rich poker-faced each other. No way out: They would have to meet this man and find out what he was up to. Rich felt his throat tighten at the thought that perhaps it was he who killed the man in the crypt. He was about to touch Simonetta's arm and whisper his suspicion but postponed it.

Be brave. Keep it to yourself.

"He wants to give me a test." Ornella took a bite of pizza and laughed. She rocked her head and pushed a napkin against her mouth, catching a mozzarella string. "I really didn't tell you what he looked like. Not really. With the fur, I mean. He has these big bushy orange sideburns. I mean, it's a beard on the side of his face. Ha ha! On the sides, like floppy ears. And a lot of hair on top. Like a fountain spraying down, you know, both sides—woosh! And a beard. He looked just like—" She laughed again. "It's really funny, no? He looked just like a lion!"

***

They decided that one or more of Ornella's friendly neighbors should be present while they waited for the Tron impostor to show up. "Preferably to include a large, muscle-bound one," Rich suggested. If "il

Grande Tron" did not make an appearance, they would leave the girl in the neighbors' care. They also decided it would be a good idea to call her sister at some point. Whatever Ornella's shortcomings, memory, as she said herself, was not one of them; when asked, she quickly recited the phone number of the *rifugio* near Cortina d'Ampezzo that her sister was staying at. Rich envied her ability with numerals. It took him forever to memorize a phone number.

As they walked to her home, Ornella rambled from shop window to shop window, from trash pail to doorway to placard, much as a leashless dog does when examining new terrain. This gave Simonetta the chance to question Rich about remarks he made earlier. "So what was all that," she asked, "all that about the female messiah you came out with? Where'd you get that?"

"Well, first of all, let me apologize for being lukewarm about this whole thing. You're right, this is going somewhere."

"See!" She swatted his arm.

"Besides being damn intriguing. Okay, you know, several things she said were familiar to me, but there was a...a mashing together of elements from unrelated sources. One thing that struck me had to do with what Uncle Leo said the other night. Remember he said there was something in the book about the cancellation of thought, thinking and not thinking?"

"Yes, I remember that."

"Well, the 'on-off' thing she spoke of reminded me of it. 'The on and the off,' she said. Remember the figure in the paintings looking one way and then the other? 'Thinking, not thinking,' she said. But this is a...an *invading* interpretation. I mean, the 'on-off' thing has been added. No, *parasitical* is the better word; it's a whole other level which she tacked onto a legitimate interpretation of Tintoretto's work. See, I'm certain this Tron impostor put into her head the ideas of Guillaume Postel. He was a French mystic, scholar, humanist."

"I don't think I've heard of him. Postel?"

"It's a bit specialized, not entirely accepted where the Tintorettos are concerned. But that's where the Christ and Mary connection comes in. I've not studied him, but from what I've read Postel was a remarkably faceted guy; he sought to unify the various Christian creeds in the post-Reformation period. Extraordinary linguist he was; orientalist, having to do with Islamic culture and language, Arabic. He believed that Venice, the Venetian state, because of its endurance and peace—relative peace—was ordained by God. And he had this...kind of... He knew this woman who worked at the *Ospedaletto*. Right. He believed she was divinely inspired and that she was his spiritual mother, a Christ figure, a messiah, who would unify the world's religions. Some of his ideas involve the Kabbalah and so forth; I don't remember it all. Anyway, it's like what she said, Ornella—the female messiah thing. Two halves of the soul, male, female. Postel believed that the maternal power or genius, will rescue, or, yes, fulfill, the male or rational side of humanity."

"H'mmm, I'm beginning to like Postel."

"The thing is... There are scholars who believe Tintoretto must have come in contact with Postel's ideas."

"Interesting."

"So I guess this lion-haired fellow must have some kind of...education, right? Not that this makes me feel any better."

"It makes me feel worse."

"Oh, another thing. Sure. That wonderful Wise Man in the painting... It may be a representation of Postel himself. It's supposed to resemble etchings or images of him."

"Wow."

"In short, what we've got here is a Postel freak. I'm imagining a sort of hippy-like, cultic guy, maybe with sociopathic, Svengali-like tendencies."

"Svengali?"

"A hypnotizer. Like John Barrymore in the movie. No, something's not right. He's up to no good, that's for sure."

"But what's with the lion-hair and all?"

"I don't know, but I'm sure that's part of his *'thing'*; you know, he's a got a *'thing'* he's into. Loves to play dress-up; probably has more than one tattoo and pierced body part; familiar with drugs; gets his victims to use drugs too, the marijuana, for example, to make them gullible, more gullible. He must think that Ornella is an excellent subject for his control, probably a much better one than he's used to. Oh, and did you notice her shaking her ass? What was all that about?"

"Maybe it's a new dance — the Tintoretto."

"But, you know..." Rich blew some air and drew in his lips. This is all kind of... Something's coming to me now... It's ringing a bell. Damn! A cult-like thing, was it, I read about? Postel was it? Somebody else? But it's so distant; I don't know if I'm imaging it or confusing it with another thing. It's really...distant."

One street away from Ornella's home, Simonetta pointed up at the *nizioleto.* "Calle Tron," she observed. Rich grunted and continued on. Then all three stood as still as statues, looking up at the slim brick arch that spanned the narrow intersection of Calle Tron and the street the girl lived on. They turned the corner, going under the arch, and staggered to a stop as Rich spread his arms to hold back his companions. Five doors ahead two people savagely thrashed each another.

"I don't believe it," Rich gushed in English.

It was Emma Mead beating up another man. A slightly built, rodent-like fellow shielded himself from her umbrella blows; but then, ducking, he rose with an audible uppercut that sent her stumbling backwards on her heels. She landed flat on her back with gnashed teeth, a twisted expression that made her beautiful face vicious-looking and ugly. She rolled over on her side and let loose a string of the vilest suggestions Rich had ever heard. Getting up, she held her lower back and exclaimed, "That's it! I'm done with this shit!" She took a final wide umbrella swipe at the smirking undersized man, a movement that made her grimace in pain. "You can keep your damn book! You can all eat shit! I'm getting the hell out of here!" Rich was stunned to see her actually foam at the mouth. Passing the three observers she halted her half-crippled stride and made a howling medusa-like face at Rich. "Oh, *you!*" He backed up and Simonetta seized the woman in mid-lunge, but not before his attacker pinched the tip of his nose. She limped away with so many F-words that he could not count them as he often counted bell tolls and stair steps.

Simonetta grasped his arms. "Are you okay?"

He fingered his snout. "Tasmania. Errol Flynn."

"What? Are you all right, Reech?"

"Her accent. She sounded like Errol Flynn. He was born in Tasmania. That was the infamous Emma Mead."

Ornella was cowering against a wall; tears in her eyes, she hugged a fat vertical drainpipe. "That's okay, dear," Simonetta reassured, putting her arm around her. "It was only a joke."

The frail-shouldered rat-man, his smirk frozen, drifted toward them, hands in the pockets of his soft-looking black leather coat. He looked oily, his face and close-trimmed stringy black hair moist and unwashed. His brown lidless eyeballs seemed painted on wood. A square white bandage patched one side of his forehead.

Ornella, whimpering and trembling, suddenly cried, *"Il diavolo! E' il diavolo lui!"*

Without removing his hands from his pockets the man slowly shrugged his shoulders, an action that shifted his coat up to his ears and down again. "No, I am not the devil," he assured in whiney nasal English, German accented but with a peculiar Mexican or perhaps Romanian twang. *"Non so-no di-a-vo-lo."*

His heart pounding, Rich clamped on a relaxed demeanor. "So what's going on?" he asked him, sticking to English.

"She knew you, that woman."

"Knew me?"

"You have met her before."

Ornella, with frenzied sobbing, broke away from Simonetta and darted around the corner into Calle Tron. She ran after her.

Don't leave me with this weirdo!

Rich curled his lip, rolled his shoulders. "Some book..."

Damn, why did I say that?

"Some *something* she wanted once. I don't know. She's a little crazy, if you want my opinion."

"I was asking in this neighborhood about a book."

Okay, calm down. Do a little research.

"What book? Why are you looking here?"

He pointed at the intersection. "Tron, Calle Tron. Too many coincidences, you see. You know, don't you?"

"I'm quite sure I don't," Rich replied, not knowing why he produced an offended British tone.

The man's pointed tongue raced across his lips; his eyes grew larger. "There are other Tron locations. The Tron Bridge. Corte Tron. A person lives there I would like to meet."

That's all!

He inched closer to Rich. "I am a rare book collector. You see, the book is about coincidences. They say it is so powerful that any coincidence with its title or with its author's name may be a clue to its location. Strange, is it not?"

"Yes. I know a few things about old books, but I really—"

"Do you know which book I mean?"

"I don't think... Is this a one-volume work or—?"

He lunged a step. "You know which book I mean?"

"You mean, uh, *Coincidence Galore* by, uh, Hugo Friedhofer?"

Damn, isn't he a composer?

He lunged again, was louder. "You know which book I mean?"

Rich replayed the British tone, realizing it was an aid to keep his cool. "I'm quite sure I don't."

Old chap.

The man horse-snorted at the ground. He grumbled in German, swore at himself or at the world. "*Verdammt!* I *had* the book," he hissed, "the one-book, the part-one book." He jabbed a finger near his forehead bandage. "It was stolen from me this morning." He glared at Rich as if he were responsible. "That Freak!"

"Freak?"

"That orange-hair freak! You know him?"

"No, I don't. Orange hair?"

He lunged a step forward. "You know him?"

Don't start that again.

"You work for Devlin Raptor? Tell me!"

"Devlin who? Raptor? I never heard of him."

"Now I need again two books you say?"

"Well, I'm really sorry, I—"

Unexpectedly the man's body jerked as if electrified; he dug his fingers into his cheeks, cried out in German and dashed around the bend into Calle Tron. Rich caught only two words—*Das Mädchen,* meaning *the girl.* He darted into the lane behind him. The women had vanished; all he saw was the back of the man; he was racing toward the Zalizada San Stae, a wider, more traveled avenue. Certainly Simonetta had ushered Ornella to this street to escape the claustrophobic lanes of the neighborhood.

Rather than chase him, Rich sprinted away in the opposite direction, sensing that Ornella's street was a useless dead end. He hoped for a roundabout way to sneak into the salizada. Immediately to his left was the Calle del Forno; but it was too long a passage; a short sprint ahead, to his right, a rusty open gate gave on to a shorter lane; and he hoped it would turn in the direction he wanted. He rushed down the narrow brick alley and into a tomato-sauce scented no-outlet cortile.

Dammit!

He trotted out a circle, chasing a cat; he retraced his steps and crossed to the long Calle del Forno, hoping its end-point would turn toward the salizada. Passing window after ancient window, door after weathered door, bricks and more bricks, his mind raced like his feet. The man said...he said... Book One was stolen from him...stolen from him this morning...by an orange-haired freak. So who cut the throat...of the man...in the crypt? For the book. Cut his throat. Must have been—

I'm chasing a murderer!

Another lane, a left turn, joined the end of the Calle del Forno. Undoubtedly it led to the Salizada di San Stae. It was narrow, with unexpected shop windows. He trotted through it; with a forced smirk he politely slid past two people, reached the end, and stopped.

What am I doing?

Panting, he fingered the fog off his eyeglasses and smoothed back his warm, moist hair. Without stepping into the wider avenue, he peered cautiously right and left, looking for Simonetta and Ornella or the ratty little man. The wall to his left bulged out; the protrusion forced him to take a couple steps into the salizada to see farther. Among the well-spaced pedestrians he saw no familiar shapes. He backed into the narrow passage. The distant rise of organ music—

Cell phones. We've got cell phones.

—brought to mind the dead man in the crypt.

He found her entry, thumbed the *Send* icon. He made his super-fast sign of the cross to fortify the chance of her answering.

"Reech!"

"Yes, where are you?"

"We're...we're..."

"Where!"

"We're in a doorway on San Stae, near Calle Tron. I just saw the man pass us. We're waiting here for a moment. He was headed— Oh no, oh no. He sees us! He sees us!"

Her phone went dead.

Rich raced into the salizada. Now he saw the toy-sized figures of the two women ahead of him; they crossed the route, Simonetta pulling Ornella by the hand. Rat Man, black leather coat flying open like a cape, swooped after them. About to cry out for help, Rich ran toward them but went speechless when in a sidelong glimpse a new sight shocked itself into his turmoil: an overgrown middle-aged gnome with great side-beards and a fount of cascading yellow-orange hair. It was the exact lion-picture Ornella conveyed of the man who declared himself Tron.

The Freak!

On top of the stunning after-image Rich saw Rat Man disappear behind the two women into a calle. As he reached the entrance to the slender, darkish slot his thoughts gasped for straws and quickly weaved themselves into a tidy tapestry.

My God, I hope I'm right about the freak. I can use him.

He was directly behind the Rat Man now, who was in touching-distance of the women; he called out to him, "No no no, wait!" He tapped his supple leather shoulders. "Listen!"

The creature spun around—a sliver blade switched out. "Get away from me!" he ordered." Rich raised his hands, backed up; he imagined the blade slitting his tender neck, his mother weeping over his julienned corpse. "The man who stole your book!" He pointed frantically behind himself. "The furry man!" He churned his hands near his head. "With all the hair, orange hair. The book-man! He's there! You must believe me!" The Rat scowled and touched the bandage on his head. "The girl has no book, nothing! She doesn't know anything! Come with me! Hurry!"

"I'll kill you if you lie."

This is not happening

"He's there, really!" He gingerly tapped the man's arm to coax him and called out in English to the women, who were at the canal-end of the dead-end lane. "It's okay. You can come. Come on." But he patted the air to suggest they keep their distance. The man glanced over his shoulder at them; with an exasperated sigh, he rubbed his face with his sleeve, reactions Rich thought showed weakness. In a flash he concealed his practiced blade. "Hurry!" Rich cried, gently cupping the man's elbow. "Follow me!"

Out in the salizada they were just in time to see Lion Man approach the entrance to Calle Tron. Rat Man screamed at him in German, shockingly loud and shrill; people looked, halted. The Lion stood still for a second as the Rat came at him; but instead of running away, the hairy character turned around, bent over and wiggled his silver-studded blue-jeaned rear-end at him.

What the hell?

Rat Man staggered to a stop, his face blank; he wobbled, squeezed his eyes shut; and an alien emotion came over Rich:

Maybe the furry fellow is just misunderstood.

The Rat closed his eyes, and as if fighting a ferocious inner urge, propelled himself with gnashed teeth and bracing battle cry at his tail-waggling enemy, who paused, looked over his shoulder and then took off down the salizada at a surprising pace. Then he stopped, looked behind him and wiggled his bottom once more, which again made Rat Man stall in his tracks. This stop-and-go act took place several times before Rich's puzzled eyes, the performance recalling a silent comedy routine.

He trotted back to Simonetta and Ornella. *"Squagliamoci!"* (Let's beat it!) he called out.

"What happened?" Simonetta asked.

"That was Tron!" Ornella cried, clinging to Simonetta.

"He calls himself Tron, Ornella, but he's not. He's no good. Like the other man. They're both no good. Remember that."

But why was he shaking his ass?

Rich noted two policemen, who had swaggered into the salizada; but, thoughts racing and colliding, he shook his head.

A short jog later they sat on the wide flat steps beneath the white baroque frosting of the Church of San Stae, near the vaporetto stop, gazing across the Grand Canal. The clean, clear spaciousness of area was a relief. Rich explained to Simonetta that the sudden sight of the lion-haired man, who was no doubt on his way to keep his meeting with Ornella, made him think of what the girl said he had told her, that he had recently found Book One. "And the ratty guy was raving about an orange-haired freak who stole it from him. So I figured it was good bet it was the Lion Man who swiped it, right? They're natural enemies."

"Well, it was quick thinking, my darling."

"It was all on *adrenalina*, somehow. It was—"

Simonetta's hands smoothed Rich's coat-front and her lips sought his, tasted his. Holding onto her ears, he pulled her closer, tighter to himself. Now Ornella jumped in; she hugged Simonetta's back and rested her head there. "Okay," Rich said, breaking it up, "church steps." He rubbed his eyes as Simonetta shot an aggrieved look at Ornella. "You know, I'm pretty sure... I'm pretty sure the Rat Man killed the guy in the crypt."

"You think?"

"That must be where he got the book in the first place. He told me he had Book One this morning."

"I'd say it's time to call the police, no? In any case, we have to tell Uncle Leo everything. He'll know how to deal with it. Do you think those two guys will kill each other?"

"God forgive me, I hope so."

The vaporetto boat came into view and the three friends filed over to the platform.

"Weird thing," Rich went on. "When the Lion Man shook his behind something happened, strange. Did you see that?"

"I'm not sure what I saw. I was in a fog. What strange?"

"It was like... Well, I saw that the ratty guy was affected, afflicted somehow. And then... I don't know... I felt... Well...I had an odd thought or feeling, like sympathy."

"We all need a rest."

Ornella broke in as she boarded the boat. "Yes, he shakes his *culo*, I know, I know," and she did her twisty dance.

Rich and Simonetta looked at each other. The girl's movements, they knew, brought to both their minds the wiggling little number she did at the Scuola.

"What is that about?" Simonetta asked the girl.

"He shakes all those shiny buttons and it says things to you. It sort of makes you think, makes you think. Different things. Once he shook I knew I liked him. It was true, what he was saying—about the paintings and himself and things."

Rich and Simonetta stared at each other and puckered their lips, but not as a prelude to a kiss.

***

"You must, tomorrow at eleven, be here at my house," Leo told Simonetta over the phone. "There's something going on and I've initiated certain actions. My phones are secure now, so we can talk. A man is here and will be here all day and all night. He can explain what's happening. I had no idea so much was happening. What I started with a simple... Well, with a prank!"

"I'll say," Simonetta sighed quietly.

"*Contributed to,* is more accurate. I spoke to you about this man before, the other night at the table. Major Worthington. The skinny-skinny fellow I let copy my book, I told you; had a little spy camera. Well, he looks different now, to say the least. We did, after all, inform certain police officials about what we know. That turned out okay. They know me. Now, tell me..."

Simonetta described to her uncle nearly all that had happened since their meeting around the dining room table two days earlier. He was not the least surprised. "I know, I know," he insisted repeatedly, "I hear what you're saying."

While Ornella dozed peacefully in an easy chair, Simonetta gave an account to Rich of her uncle's comments.

"*Madonna,*" he sighed, massaging his neck. "What have we gotten ourselves into? Did he mean his phones were tapped?"

"I think so. Anyway, tomorrow will prove interesting."

Ornella's cell phone played a disco song and woke her up. It was her sister. Simonetta went over to the girl, as she thought it a good idea to speak with her relative about the well-being of her wayward sibling when the opportunity was right.

All during Simonetta's conversations, Rich paced around quietly and dreamily. He was receiving his flecks, those life-charged nanosecond flashes in which he sometimes became poetically absorbed. The usual stimuli — among which he counted late-day light, light-and-shade divisions and certain musical harmonies — did not so much cause the present flecks; rather they rushed to him as deliverances from the strain of recent anxiety. He was familiar with this compensatory reaction and knew it to be a healing balm. When he sat down, the exquisite flecks continued to manifest themselves in tiny intermittent instances; the inspiration, he thought, was the Bavarian-looking pizza place they visited earlier in the day; except it had transformed itself into a lodge or chalet, tucked away in the snowy Alps.

Real life is there.

"Well, that was a little knotty at first," Simonetta lamented as she sat down with a huff next to Rich.

"I'm Sorry. You said?"

"I spoke to Ornella's sister, and...let's say I resolved it all. I made up a chance-encounter story." She yawned and stretched. "It's okay. She's wandered into situations before."

Real life is there.

"Did you hear me?"

"It's okay? Oh, it's okay. Yes, I heard you. Great."

"She's glad the kid is in good hands. She's telling the neighbors so that they don't worry. Oh, she said she thinks somebody slipped a drug or something into her lemonade the night she saw the monster. Some creep at the party they were at."

Real life.

"You're in one of your otherworldly trances, I think."

"I've got a poem in me, sorry."

"She and her husband will be back tomorrow at noon. I'll take her home in the morning. A neighbor will meet us."

"Uh huh. He looked at Ornella, who was now on the floor, her face in a magazine, and then faced Simonetta. "Not otherworldly, though. Not really. You, you're on the down-side of manic this evening."

"Tired." She yawned again. "Excuse me. Remember this morning I was dancing on air?"

"Right, and I was...animated. Animatedly reflective."

"You were pulling me around like a *pazzo. O Merda!* I've got to see my assistant, Luciana, at the office. I've been neglecting my paper. Got to call my parents too."

"I missed calling my mother today." You said the ads are way down, after the carnival."

"Yes, but still. Bah, I'm not thinking about it now."

She pressed her cheek into his shoulder and slid her hand up the arm of his soft gray cashmere sweater.

He voiced in English, "Carved like cuckoo clocks these Bavarian chambers."

She lifted her head. "What?"

"That'll be the first line of my poem. Wait a second." He leaned forward, disengaging her, and slid a pad and pencil toward himself on the coffee table. He wrote down his first line, tore it from the pad, and stuffed it into his pocket. "Sometimes a place appears in my flecks or flashes. It's a place in a time, an age, charged—shocked—with real life. *Real* life. This one happens to be nice and cozy." He snickered. "I notice now it's changing into flecks of my room at home, in Rhode Island." He sighed. "Me too, I forgot all about calling mom," he repeated. "Oh well, look, I better get back to my place." He stood up. "I'll tinker with my poem, get my mind off all this...stuff. I think this meeting with Leo and this Worthington fellow *will* be interesting. Relax tonight. I'm sure you'll be dancing on air again tomorrow."

Simonetta sat back, arms folded. "Real life," she mused, half to herself. "I guess we don't have that around here."

***

Even under foggy, sour window light it was obvious that the man in the soft black leather coat was caked green and red with algae. The side of his forehead where the bandage had been, and the whole side of his face, was also matted green and red—but more with the red of blood than with stringy slime. Four rats nibbled at his eyes, two per socket, as his stiff legs scissored slowly in the black, freezing water. A motorboat pilot, having unwittingly dragged the corpse for half a kilometer, had just as unwittingly beached it on the slimy steps of the Rio della Pergola. An icy cry from a window had opened other windows and soon the police were on the scene. They transferred the corpse to a shiny black bag and boated the bloated body away.

Chapter Three

Rich planned to spend the morning indoors with his poem until ten and leave at that hour for Campo Santa Maria Formosa, where he and Simonetta agreed to meet before heading to Leo's. But an anxious thought had seized him in his sleep and chased away the evening's poetic enchantment: Perhaps it would be wise to accompany Simonetta on her way to take Ornella home. At eight forty-five he called her and offered to meet them.

"No, Reech. It's okay. We left my place a few minutes ago. I'll give you a ring when I drop her off."

"Are you sure?"

"Yes, I'll ring you on my way back."

But at nine o'clock a call from her forced him out of the house, for a completely unexpected reason.

"Reech, Reech, you must see this!"

"Oh no, what is it now?"

Her voice was breathy. "This is really, really strange, Reech!"

"Come on, Simonetta! What is it? You okay?"

"I don't want to scare Ornella so I'm keeping it down. Okay, so we leave my place and walk into Campo San Bartolomio. That's where we are now. Listen to this!"

"I'm listening, I'm listening!"

"In the middle of the campo, there's this guy. He's all dressed up in, like, Renaissance clothes, or Commedia dell'Arte clothes, with the half-mask, you know, like in a Goldoni play."

"Okay, okay—carnival stuff, like that."

"Yeah, so, he's talking and talking, like he's preaching and lecturing, and next to him is a stand-up placard. The placard says in big letters on top..." She swallowed.

"What? What?"

"It says, 'Leonardo Tron and The Living Roots of Possibility,' and then 'Quantum Physics in the sixteenth century.' Reech, you hear me? Are you there?"

"I'm here." He saw his own thinking face.

"It's like an advertisement for a performance or play or something. There's a performance time and today's date on the bottom. There's an address, a theater I've never heard of."

"Can you talk to the guy?"

"I can't. I'm walking and talking. I'm running late. You need to come here. You can grill him when he shuts up, if he ever does. We'll meet later as planned. Leave now!"

"Okay, I will. Be careful!"

They hung up. He tossed a warning at the deaf-and-dumb phone, "Scan the lanes for weirdoes," he said in English. He grabbed his coat and went out into the chilly, partly cloudy morning.

What was to have been a ten- or fifteen-minute walk came to an end after only five. Before him in the airy Campo Daniele Manin, right under the monument to the patriot himself, and in front of the hefty ready-to-fly bronze lion, stood a lecturing man dressed like the one Simonetta described having seen in Campo San Bartolomio. His garb was of a dandified courtier, with a lot of white ruffles at the neck and sleeves, a plumed hat, and a half-mask. At a distance Rich noted the "Leonardo Tron" placard like the one she had read to him. Other strollers cast glances at the man. He examined people with a furtive, staccato alertness.

Rich's cell phone rang and he pulled it from his pocket.

"Simonetta?"

"Reech! Listen to this."

"No, wait a minute, you listen to me."

"No no, hear this! We're at the Rialto *imbarcadèro*. There's the *same kind of guy* preaching over here. Like the guy in San Bartolomio. He's got the Tron sign and everything."

"Holy smoke!" Rich cried in English. "There's a guy right here in front of me in Campo Manin doing the same damn thing."

"What! Oh oh, wait a second! Oh oh oh oh...!"

"What, what, what?"

"Across the Canalazzo! I'm looking across" — she gave an eel squeal — "there's *another one!* He's near the bridge!"

"Okay, okay, let me study my guy here. Again, be careful. And don't scare Ornella."

Adjusting an amicable grin, he approached the tall, lanky man but kept his distance, imitating a half-committed but still-curious passerby. The speaker interrupted his surveillance of the area and fixed his attention on Rich. He removed his feathered tricorn hat and bowed deeply with a sweeping flourish.

"*Illustrissimo signore,*" he called out, I beg your kind regard in a matter of mystery." The man's Italian was modern, but he used the plural pronoun *voi (you)* in the singular, which gave his speech an antiquated affectation. "I introduce you to a principle from the first book of Tron, by Leonardo Tron, who is a marvel of the Sixteenth Century, master of consciousness, whose practical application of theories not formulated until centuries after his time, are the subject of my discourse. *Clarissimo signore,* I give you two phenomena — wave and particle. I repeat, we have a broad wave" — he made a swimming motion with two open hands before him — "and particle" — now he poked the air several times with a finger. "So, let us imagine, you are rowing down your neighborhood rio when into your mind, for whatever reason, comes the memory of a friend, one you have not seen or even thought about in a long, long time. 'Dear Giovanni,' you say to yourself, 'I wonder what became of the old rascal.' Then, as you go about the pressing affairs of the day, the thoughts of Giovanni dissolve into the background of your life, as thoughts often do. Ah, but later that evening, or perhaps the next day, whom do you see strolling through your neighborhood campo? Who may even knock on your door? Yes, it's your long-lost chum Giovanni!

"You see: First the wave, then the particle. The broad wave — containing, let us say, the idea of Giovanni in possibility or potential — has led to the consummation, the actualization of this possibility in the Giovanni-particle; that is, in an event of tangible reality. Remember now" — he swayed back and forth — "the wave and the particle, the wave and the particle..."

Rich had a flashback of Ornella in the Scuola saying "the on and the off, the on and the off," but unlike her the loquacious cavalier did not wiggle his bottom.

"Now, *caro signore,* let us go back. The thought of Giovanni comes into your head. But because Giovanni is, let us say, a bothersome person who, let us further imagine, is always hitting you up for *scudi,* you most assuredly do not wish to encounter him. What to do? Well, consider the sudden thought you had of him. Even though an external reminder may have caused the initial thought, the idea still has a broad 'out-of-the-blue' character that raises your learned suspicion that one of those startling coincidences *might* come of it. Once you have this suspicion, and, most important, say 'This will *not* be one of *those* coincidences,' and blink your eyes to delineate your command, you will not meet up with the bothersome Giovanni!

"Now, you ask, 'What has happened?' What science is behind the prevention of 'Giovanni-the-Realized-Particle,' so to speak?"

The man relaxed, went out of character. He politely waved for Rich to come closer. He took from his embroidered pocket several of sheets of paper. "I didn't have time to memorize the rest," he confided, sounding more Southern Italian, perhaps Neapolitan, than he had before, "so I'm going to read it."

"What are you advertising?" Rich asked. "Is it a lecture?"

"Oh, it's a lecture, I think. Yes, a lecture. The place and time are on the sign." Again the man scanned the area closely. Rich noted that the event was at eight o'clock this evening in the sestiere of Dorsoduro at a theater he had never heard of.

"I memorized all that, what you just heard," the man confided. "Not bad for two hours work, wouldn't you say?"

"Yes, you're good. Who's behind this program, do you know? Who wrote your text, put together your discourse?"

As other strollers approached, the man began again, now reading from his typewritten pages. "*Illustrissimi Signori,* here we are several centuries later in a scientific laboratory more advanced than Tron could have imagined, but where subatomic experiments curiously reflect his writings. Remember from before: wave and particle...wave and particle. Picture a thin wall of, say, one or two meters square. It sits on a desk or a pedestal, whichever you prefer. In the wall are two narrow slits, well separated, either horizontal or vertical, it makes no difference. A few meters behind the wall stands another wall; this one is coated with a registering agent, like photographic film, and is completely blank. Now we close one slit in the first wall; then we use a marvelous contraption to fire a series of electron particles through the one open slit. When we examine the second wall we find just what we expected: the electrons left a concentrated pattern on the wall matching the shape of the slit we fired them through, as if we had shot grains of sand through it and onto a sticky background. Now we wipe clean the second wall of our experiment, and open the second slit in the first wall, giving the electrons, so to speak, a choice of which slit to go through. However, after sending them through, we do not get a double-slit pattern on the second wall, as we would expect.

Instead we get a wave pattern—a series of bands, a broad wave band actually, that joins the two locations—as if we had sent a liquid or light through the slits; that is, it appears that all the fluid-like expansion, interferences and canceling-out one would expect with a liquid or 'broader' agent has now happened with discrete electron particles. How can this be? After all, are not electrons individual things?"

The most recently arrived spectators went on their way, apparently bored with or uninterested in the man's discourse, though other potential arrivals wandered here and there around the campo, glancing at the show. "I'm losing my audience," the speaker confided, "would you like me to continue?"

"Oh yes, please do, I find it interesting. Are you an actor? Whose lecture is this? Who's behind the event?"

The man looked all around to see whether more people entered the campo. "Yes, an actor, from an agency." He began again, "Okay, where was I? To tell the truth, I don't know what the hell I'm reading. *Va bene...* So the electrons surprisingly made a wave-band pattern instead of a double-slit pattern." He resumed his reading. "Now, the question is, could the electron particles have somehow interfered with one another as they passed through the two slits, thus creating the unexpected wave pattern on the second wall? Well, why don't we shoot one electron through at a time? This way they cannot possibly touch one another. We do so, making sure the time between firings is well spaced. But, still, after they all go through, we end up with a wave pattern rather than a two-slit pattern! *Stranissimo! Bizzaro, infatti!* What is going on? How can one-at-a-time electrons interfere with themselves and make a wave pattern as if they were light waves or a liquid?

"Now, since we were not able, of course, to watch the subatomic particles go through the slits, let us set up an observation device to determine what is happening when the particles go through. Well, one thing we find is about half the electrons pass through one slit and half pass through the other. Very well, that's normal. But wait! Another strange thing has happened! Instead of getting the inexplicable wave-pattern on the second wall, as before, we see the logically expected particle-pattern, which matches the two slits. The electrons have returned to behaving like particles instead of like a wave! What's going on? In experiment after experiment it turns out—ah!—that when we *observe* the electrons going through the two open slits *they behave like particles* and when we do not observe them *they behave like waves.* It is as if our attention—the use of our conscious minds—collapses the wave into the 'specificity' of particles! Our *mental presence* appears to give the particles a *specific expected behavior,* stopping their bizarre, seemingly impossible wave-performance. This tells us something we have suspected for a while, that without our watching—without our conscious presence—each individual electron was free to choose all possibilities, not only one slit but both at the same time!

"Does each electron actually go through both slits at once when the 'filter' of our consciousness is not present? Could the particles interact with past and future particles? More broadly, when are you not observing, does the world—does your bedroom or bathroom when you are not there—exist in a non-entity state of infinite possibility or probability awaiting your senses to actualize it, to create its specific being? He shook his papers noisily. "How do you answer *that?*" he asked, ad-libbing.

"I've read about this recently," Rich said. "It's called *L'esperimento della doppia fenditura*" (the double-slit experiment).

"A scholar here! I can tell by the spectacles."

He kept on reading, rotating a finger, becoming more comically flamboyant to ease his tedium. "I repeat—as prefigured in Tron's way of seeing—that the wave, behind our back, so to speak, is a non-thing containing all possibilities at once—that is, when our mind is *not* present. The particle, on the other hand, is a fully realized individualized instance of reality derived from those unlimited possibilities, a reality that happens as soon as our mind *is* present. So when...when that...pain-in-the-ass Giovanni comes into your mind—which is to say, when the pristine initial thought of him is in your mind as a candidate for birth as a coincidence—as an unstudied wave of limitless potential—*uff!*—you can negate that potential, and thwart its consummation in reality, by wedging in a mind-command, namely, 'This will not be one of *those* coincidences.' Tron asks you to blink here. If you execute this command, *your mind conscious of itself* empties the wave of—cancels out—its Giovanni-potential by 'particle-izing' the initial and sudden Giovanni-thought into a simple and constrained 'thought-about thought,' which involves recognizing it for the coincidence it might have become, a recognition that negates the thought's initial power or possibility-potential. *Dio mio!* In other words, the primal Giovanni-thought now loses its freedom in the realm of the possible, just as the electrons, when we observe them, lose their freedom to make every choice.

Therefore you can shout *addio* to the Giovanni-coincidence that...might have been born...from the fertile wave...of the possible. In short..."

The man was laughing, quietly bordering on mock-hysteria.

"In short and in general...our consciousness...fulfills the outcome of all things...or...in the case at hand...the *non-encountered-outcome* of that...that smarmy little bastard known as Giovanni! *Addio, Giovannaccio!*" The man bowed deeply.

Rich lightly applauded.

"Sorry, this is my tenth reading today."

"*Ben fatto! Bravo!*"

"*Vi ringrazio.* At least I'm getting well paid. Oh wait, *scusate*, there's more." He cleared his throat, stiffened up. "At this evening's event you will not only hear how to cancel unwanted coincidences, as described early in Book One, but will also get a preview of Book Two, in which a method of *creating* coincidences is thoroughly explained! *Ecco tutto.*"

Book Two. Creating coincidences. No way.

Rich was about to ask again who was responsible for putting on the lecture program, but the man effected a dramatic bird-flight posture at the sight of three more people approaching. "*Illustrissimi signori,*" he cried out, beginning all over again. Rich assumed that either the man did not know the answer to his question or someone had instructed him not to reply.

Rich traipsed away in a mental whirlpool.

So that's what Tron's thesis is all about, he contemplated. It's like quantum physics. Or, at least, someone has found in it a parallel with quantum physics.

But what's going on with these people?

He began to perceive a connection between Jung's theory of synchronicity—causeless coincidence—and quantum physics, a controversial subject involving the uncanny behavior of sub-atomic particles in relation to one's conscious awareness of them.

Who wrote this stuff?

Resuming his usual rapid gait, he passed along the left side of the modern savings bank, on the north end of Campo Manin, and into Campo San Luca, where he had first seen pugnacious Emma Mead reflected in a bookstore window. Now a new sight seized him: in the center of the campo stood another lecturing courtier.

Are they everywhere?

He advanced toward the speaker. To his surprise, he preached in English. The discourse was mostly the same as the first one he heard, but new points came to light in the current version, which the man read from typewritten pages. "Tron suggests that after saying or thinking 'this will not be one of *those* coincidences,' the command be followed by a blinking of the eyes. The blinking has no power in itself; in fact, some people spit; others expel wind; it is only a comfort, a confirmation that the command has been executed. This can be called *'clicking off,'* which is to say that you have 'clicked off' or banished the possibility of a coincidence by adopting conscious intrusion. So it is with the audible click of typewriter or keyboard keys, which sound does nothing in itself except assure the typist that letters have been registered. Likewise Tron claims that the magic wands about which we read in the tales of wizards, never do anything in themselves when waved or tapped, as the naïve reader thinks, but are nothing more than a physical reassurance the wizard provides himself, confirming the performance of a mental command."

Familiar repetitions followed, so Rich left for Campo San Bartolomio. It was from there that Simonetta, on her way to take Ornella home, called in the news of her first sighting.

All at once the darkness of worry:

Maybe I should have insisted on going with her.

Suppose they run into Rat Man or Lion Man? He zipped a whisking sign of the cross to drive away the possibility. At that moment he realized with a strange calmness that his sign-of-the-cross habit was analogous to the canceling-out 'command' both speakers had referred to.

Interesting...

He went off on an idea excursion, musing.

Analogous, yes, but not exact.

His was a physical reinforcement, yes, of a thought, but also a dispatched request for the realization or negation of this thought in reality. It was also a communication asking that a thing or situation be fortified with a blessing.

Still, there's a connection here.

He wondered whether some religious acts had their roots in quantum physics.

I'll have to ponder this in bed some night.

He took out his phone to call Simonetta. It rang in his hand. "Simonetta! I found another guy, in Campo San Luca!"

"I found another one too! In front of San Stae. Very strange, Reech! You know, you know, I'm wondering..."

"You're wondering?"

"No, we'll talk later, later. I just dropped off Ornella, left her with a couple of neighbors."

"Good. She'll be okay."

"Sweet people. That's a relief. They gave me a nice piece of mozzarella to take home."

"You'll be safer without her now. Mozzarella?"

"I wanted to say let's meet at Uncle Leo's House instead of waiting for each other in Santa Maria Formosa."

"Why don't we meet at the Rialto? I'm right nearby. We can walk together from there."

"I'm afraid I'd be late. That Worthington man he wants us to meet..."

"Late by a few minutes maybe, that's all. It's best we go together."

"Okay, it's five after ten now. I'll meet you at the foot of the bridge, San Marco side, ten thirty or so, between ten-thirty and ten forty-five. Then we'll make a dash for it. "

"Okay, be careful. Put your hood up."

He hung up and frowned at the lecturer, who incessantly spouted his esoteric treatise. He left the campo, not knowing where to rest his wits. He thought back to when his phone rang; he wondered what would have happened—or not happened—if the thought of her calling had come into his mind before she called, and if, before she called, he had "clicked it off" saying "this is not going be a coincidence"— would she have actually called?

This is like a video game in your head.

He rushed down the Calle del Teatro and into long and relatively narrow Campo San Bartolomio, with its eclectic series of many-windowed facades and its amused-looking statue of playwright Carlo Goldoni. Under the congenial, smiling figure, the man whom Simonetta first reported still bleated his oration.

Wait a minute. Could Leo be behind all this?

He gazed up at Goldoni, who now looked like a smirking smart-ass.

Is that what Simonetta was wondering? Maybe he's trying to trap somebody. No, that's too much, really too much. Still...

The latest lecturer, a chubby fellow with a full black beard, held the attention of at least a dozen people, tourists included. His main lecture was like the others, but after a while he too touched on points Rich had not heard before.

"In addition to the cancellation of a possible and straightforward coincidence," he went on, "we have the ironic or reversal mode. This is when you make a forceful statement, often a judgment or prideful boast, and the opposite happens. 'Our team will surely devastate the other!' and you lose miserably. 'I predict we will have spectacular weather next Tuesday!' and it rains buckets. Or you indulgently comment on how beautiful a building is and then, the next day, it burns down."

The look-ma-no-hands mode.

"There are also the trickster-like substitutions or symbolic consummations that may await a condition or event, as it is with the tightrope walker who before a challenging performance, of which he is particularly fearful, slips on his front steps and breaks his neck. Had he properly 'clicked off' the idea of an ironic daily-life variant of a rope accident, he would have particle-ized the wave-thought into a normal thought and neutralized the tragic realization in its dormant ironic seed."

Okay, that's enough. Clear your head.

But as he made for the Rialto Bridge, he thought back years before to what his great-grandmother had told him about certain behaviors she remembered or had heard of as a child in Southern Italy. She told him that people would sometimes rub dirt on their children's faces and deliberately ruffle their clothes to make them unattractive to others. This was because they feared that if their kids looked nice they might receive compliments, and such flattery might damn their natural good looks or well-being. They might lose their beauty through, say, disfigurement in an accident or another way.

And even now some think wishing 'buona fortuna' is bad.

He paused at the foot of the Rialto Bridge.

'Break a leg,' they say to actors, wishing the opposite. Could that somehow be like primitive sacrifice?

He shook off his thoughts as dog shakes off rain.

Gimme a break! Peasants toiling with sub-atomic particles! My great-great-grandfather juggling electrons…

He glanced at his watch.

Very tiny great-great grandfather.

It was nearly ten-thirty. He looked around, paced. He spied in the distance the other Tron lecturer that Simonetta mentioned, the one near the vaporetto stop.

Am I living in a dream or what? Maybe I died or something. If you die do you know it?

His phone rang. It was Simonetta. "Ciao," he greeted. "Let me tell you —"

"*San Stae, mozzarella, pezzpaterra,*" she sputtered in a urgent-sounding voice; then the call dropped.

"What? *Pronto?* Simonetta?" He called her back, got her voicemail, but hung up.

What did she say?

San Stae, mozzarella, pezzpaterra. He thought for a moment. Okay, maybe she's back at the San Stae church; that's good; Ornella's nice neighbors gave her some mozzarella. I knew that. What's *pezzpaterra* mean? *Pezzo* is *piece; terra* is *earth* or *ground. Pezzpa?* What's that? *Paterra? Pezzpaterra? Earth pieces? Ground pieces?* Though he had studied Italian since he was ten, he still encountered words and expressions he had forgotten through disuse or could not remember having seen or heard before.

Whatever. She'll call back.

He spent the next ten minutes with one eye on the windows of clothing stores, restaurants, and souvenir shops near the foot of the bridge, and the other eye on pedestrians.

Come on, Simonetta, hurry it up.

Five minutes later and still no Simonetta.

Ever more self-conscious, he leaned against a corner wall, took out his Smartphone to pass the time with the online news.

What the hell is this!

He pulled off his glasses and moved his phone close to his eyes to examine the photo, catching peripherally the headline: *Trovato corpo nel Rio della Pergola (Body Found in the Della Pergola Canal).* No doubt: It was the passport photo of the character he and Simonetta called Rat Man. Rich read, *Frozen, mutilated body... Suspicious German passport...* There were rumors of a link with a covered-up killing in a tourist location.

Rich took out his phone, found Simonetta's name and hit *Send.* Her phone rang three, four, five times; then her voicemail. "Simonetta. It's almost ten to eleven. I'm at the bridge. Call me back, okay? Where are you? I just read something in the news... You have to see it. Okay." He looked at the photo of Rat Man again and shivered at the filthy memory of him.

God, I wonder...I wonder if Lion Man...got him.

Bells tolled deliriously on the Saint Mark side of town. Eleven o'clock and still no Simonetta. He phoned her again.

Maybe her battery went dead. Yes. But why is she late?

Then it was five after. Ten after. He paced. He smoked. His mouth went dry. His blood raced. Then it was quarter after. He called her, got the same five interminable rings and her message. He felt light, had the sensation of being one giant floating eyeball.

She's dead. That's all. Lion Man got her. She's dead.

He wished he had Leo's number. *Simonetta's not answering, Leo. I don't know where she is. What should I do?* He knew that Leo had his number. He hoped he would call when finally he missed them.

Little eel, where are you?

He imagined Simonetta hanging by chains, Simonetta on the rack, Simonetta prodded with red-hot pokers...

Click it off... This is not going to be one of those thought-coincidences...! Click it off... Oh I'm losing my mind!

He made the sign of the cross, a properly slow one.

Out of nowhere the old saying 'speak of the devil,' spitefully forced itself word for word into his mind. His face burned at the thought that this saying was applied to coincidences.

Maybe Tron is the devil.

His heart beat in his ears as he watched a man in sixteenth-century attire climb the side-steps to the bridge; he was apparently the one who was speaking at the vaporetto stop. He smoked an out-of-period cigarette and had the carefree air of someone leaving work. Another man in garb appeared, sauntering down the central ramp; he was probably the lecturer Simonetta noticed on the San Polo side of the canal.

The dandy continued straight and merged with people in the connecting salizada.

His phone rang.

"Oh thank God!"

He pulled it from his coat pocket and fumbled with it, watched it somersault on his fingertips. He dropped it, stuck out his foot to break its fall and caught it as it touched his boot.

"*Pronto?*" he answered still bent over.

"*Carlo?*" asked the voice.

"*Carlo? No, no, ha sbagliato numero.* Dammit!"

He did a nervous two-step, one step toward the bridge, the other away from it, unsure about whether to run to Leo's or —

Pezzpaterra. San Stae, mozzarella, pezzpaterra.

"Pezzi per terra! Pieces on the ground!"

A moving image of Simonetta rippled through his mind. Her hand was dipping in and out of her coat pocket, breaking off small bits of the mozzarella that Ornella's neighbors had given her and dropping them on the pavement, leaving a trail.

Yes, that sounds just like her, but...

No buts — it was weird enough to be true. He climbed the central ramp of the bridge, searching his mind for a route to the Salizada San Stae and the church of the same name. It was not clear to him how to get there from the bridge; the intervening calli were a jumble in his memory. He thought he should take the fish-market route, along the Grand Canal, since the Church of San Stae was on the canal itself and not far from there; but he failed to recall whether this route followed through along the water or detoured away from it into the labyrinth of streets. He sensed the latter was true but chose it just the same; he would be closer to his destination and there was the chance this passage led to a nearby shortcut.

It didn't; and he wondered if 'clicking off' this undesired discovery beforehand would have caused a more direct route to appear; would have altered the structure of Venice itself, changed it on every map, throughout history, in some parallel universe that he would suddenly and seamlessly be a part of.

In the present reality, however, he needed to turn south, away from the canal. At the end of the long Calle del Campaniel he came to Campo San Cassan and from there, after scooting across the square, reversed himself and pressed on instinctively northwest through tight brick lanes and over unfamiliar bridges. He crossed himself when he reached Calle Dei Morti—Street of the Dead—adding a triple-blink and the words "click it off, click off a possible coincidence, click it off." Then, looking up, he saw a small orange *Ca' Pesaro* sign with an arrow beneath it. Good. He knew the Ca' Pesaro museum of modern art was the next important Grand-Canal building before San Stae. Soon he was at the side entrance of the museum. There at the foot of the brick bridge he skidded on something and did a kind of pirouette to keep from falling; he converted this move into an unorthodox stretching exercise to avoid embarrassment before a loitering museum visitor. He crossed the bridge, dashed down the Calle Pesaro, and at the next angle knew where he was: at the sotopòrtego along the narrow canal by the San Stae church.

He paused to collect himself. He still felt spacey, detected a rapid tremor in his head and hands.

What am I doing? Suppose she's at the Rialto!

Resolved, though, he took a step forward—and saw his boot press down on a raised white spot.

No, no way.

He lifted his toe and saw on the pale stone-block pavement a white putty-like patty the size of an American silver dollar.

No, no way.

He bent down and peeled it up. It behaved like mozzarella. He kneaded the piece between his fingers, sniffed it repeatedly.

Omigod, it is mozzarella.

He scanned the pavement for more. He advanced about ten paces under the covered passage and saw another piece.

This-is-a-maz-ing.

He retraced his steps a few paces around the corner to see if he unknowingly had followed the path in reverse. He found another piece. Now, with a bloodhound's absorption, he hunted the route he had just taken. Another piece. Then another, another... He prowled over the Ca' Pesaro bridge, saw the smeared piece he slipped on, and continued along the fondamenta. Then he turned left where he had made a right.

About five minutes later he followed the cheese around an unfamiliar bend into a chilly elbow-scraping passage that smelled of fish-trash and cat urine. The lane became a stubby, smoky-dark sotopòrtego. The cloudy jade tint and the brick wall beyond it showed that the lane stopped at a canal. Only one turn-off left him with the hope that the cheese did not stop at the water.

"Oh, crap."

The cheese continued on, through the tunnel and to the canal. He hunched over to keep from scraping his head on the low *sotopòrtego* roof.

Oh my God, He drowned her. He drowned my little eel.

The undisturbed waterway was only about three gondolas wide. Facing him across it was a square, partly opened wire grate, definitely an entrance; this rusty off-kilter hatch was at the bottom of a perplexity of crooked bricks, patches of old marble, white stone blocks, and diagonal metal braces that held it all together. An out-of-place *s'ciopon*, a narrow shallow-water rowboat popular with bird-hunters, was parked just to the left of the chaos. He looked down at the water for pieces of the milky white cheese, noting reflections he would love to photograph, and then lifted his eyes to the wide, deformed stone step across the canal at the bottom of the grate. He squinted.

"Mozzarella!"

A real sprinkling of it.

He exhaled and dropped his shoulders. Without crossing the water, how long would it take, he wondered, to get to the other side of the anonymous building? If he could even find it!

Instantly several burley, confident policemen rushed to his aid down the narrow passage behind him—in his imagination.

And tell them what? Follow the Yellow Brick Road?

With a glazed face he looked around. At his left he saw two thin steel or aluminum mooring poles sticking out of the water at an angle. He had never much noticed this kind; they were different from the thick raw-wood ones or the happily striped *paline* most observed around the city. He wondered how securely planted these were. If he jumped and grabbed a pole near the top perhaps his weight would slowly tilt it over the slender canal, at which angle, with arm- and leg-propulsion, he might toss himself into the little boat on the other side.

He saw his mother adding tears to his waterlogged corpse.

Come on, mom!

He ventured out onto the shelf-like step that jutted before him.

My corpse, sure. That's assuming they'd find me.

He moved to the edge of the step and noticed an outcropping of stone he could step on for height.

Who knows where I'd float to.

He pressed his foot to the stone spur and, arm raised, was about to test the sturdiness of the pole when he heard a sputtering behind him. He backed off. A motorized *sandòlo* boat carrying two teenage boys slowly advanced. He waved both hands at them. They looked up with anxious open faces, as if they had done something wrong, and slowed to a halt.

"Sorry, I'm lost. My grandmother is sick —

Click it off! My grandmother is not sick!

—and I have to get to the other side. Can you...?"

The boys relaxed, shrugged their permission.

"*Mille grazie.* Just over to the boat is good. I can take it from there." He stepped in. The boys used a short oar-like piece of wood against the near wall to push their idling vessel across to the parked boat. "*Tante grazie! Vi ringrazio! Siete molto gentili!*" He stepped into the other boat, took out his wallet and handed the boys ten euro. They accepted it with open-mouthed gratitude. It was an understandable reaction, since a *traghetto* ferry trip across the Grand Canal itself cost a mere two euro. As they pulled away he looked at the floor of the shabby craft and saw an ample sprinkling of path-marking mozzarella.

He grasped a drain pipe and stretched a leg out of the boat and onto the ledge-step. He pushed open the wire-grate door and moved into a weedy space that was faintly lighted from an opening above. The small refuse of a construction site littered the place. It smelled of brick-dust, old wood, wet earth. He minced his way through a doorless opening and was in another cluttered room the size of a large walk-in closet.

It was the red-brick and water-filtered light from the arched window above his head that snatched him from the present: his poetic flecks flecked through him, making life and the world wide with the breathingly joyous hints of an eternal summer-life beyond ordinary time that nevertheless contained all the times of life.

No no! Move on, you! Simonetta is in trouble!

A huge gutted room with no floors above, the underside of an ancient staircase—the whole place littered with boards, shards, mounds of gray destruction-dust all dimly lighted from high windows and smelling of rotten wood and pulverous stone— engulfed him, shrank him; but before his next breath he heard a reverberating female voice: *"Abasso le stendipanni!"*

Simonetta? Yes! That's her!

"Abasso le corde stendipanni!"

That's her. What's she saying?

Her voice came from above and behind him near his point of entry. He stifled the urge to call out; he crept to the nearest side of the room, moving along the wall next to the staircase.

"Abasso le stendipanni!"

'Down with clotheslines!' Why would she say that?

He crept closely around the front of the staircase and peered up. On the remaining piece of what was once a second floor, or perhaps a gallery, in the light of the upper windows, Simonetta sat in a simple chair, while several meters in front of her the clownish-looking Lion Man wiggled his silver-studded blue-jeaned behind much in the manner Rich had witnessed the first time he saw him.

"Forza lavanderie!" ("Up with Laundromats!") Simonetta cried.

What the hell do I do now?

Without warning, a frightfully loud horn blast and white light blurred his vision; he ducked as glass broke above, behind him, rained on him; things—big black rubbery chunks—sailed down from windows—human-shaped hunks on long black cords as someone savagely clasped him from behind and wrapped, wrapped, wrapped him tight with tape and pushed him hard into the dust as he saw two more rubber hunks sail down from the upper level, one cradling Simonetta, the other grasping the nape of dangling and fully bound Lion Man, whose fake hair hung off to reveal a startled, crooked-toothed, middle-aged derelict. His look echoed in Rich's mind: shamefully, it was an evil-looking version of the gentle, awe-inspired Wise Man in Tintoretto's nativity scene.

"Down with clotheslines, up with laundromats," Rich mumbled as he drifted puzzled into a surreal and then deep black pit.

Chapter Four

Major Worthington set down his glass of heavy cream and adjusted his two hundred and seventy pin-striped pounds in the plush Rococo settee, furniture which occupied a cozy alcove off a kind of war-room set up in Leo's house: long central table with people at laptops, maps on walls, stacks of printouts all around and NASA-types in shirtsleeves murmuring in huddles.

"I must compliment your uncle," he beamed in English with a hefty British voice. "Quite an achievement to launch such an operation, a huge—and hugely theatrical—publicity campaign for a non-existent event, inside less than twenty-four hours."

"Too bad my niece got in the way," Leo added hoarsely. "We could have got him quickly."

"The period costumes, the fine translations and adaptations of my rambling texts. To say nothing of the... What did you call those chaps?"

"*Squadra SWAT,*"

"Yes, and on the job within *three* hours! Ah, private enterprise! Leo, you should be proud of yourself."

"Cost me a fortune. I hoped to avoid such a maneuver. We could have had him without violence." Leo noticed Rich touching the square bandage on his chin. "Sorry, Rich," he said softly, with a slight chuckling sigh. He closed his eyes and stretched out his legs. "I should have called you, warned you."

"That's okay. You were busy. At least Simonetta, and my eyeglasses, emerged unscathed—I mean physically. You're sure she'll be all right? I mean, you know, in the head? She sounded pretty strange, Leo. I'm really worried about her."

Worthington reassured him: "In an hour or so all those bizarre convictions will be out of her." He thrust a match to the end of his cigar and puffed. "She'll recall it"—he blew smoke and shook out the match—"as one recalls a dream."

"My doctor is very capable," Leo murmured.

Rich looked at the black-and-white video-prints of the "Lion Man," whose name he now knew was Goodman Friendly. Two showed him menacingly arm in arm with Simonetta. He tossed them down on a side table. "Yes, uh, so..." He flashed his palms and then cupped his hands together in his lap.

"Indeed," Worthington concurred. "Doubtless I should start at the beginning. Mysteries abound for you, young man."

"I'll say," Rich grumbled; "murderers, Tintorettos, rear-end wigglers, clothesline-something-or-other. It's like peeling an onion. What was she raving about? Clotheslines, laundromats?"

"Ah! I shall spare you the tears, my boy, and peel the onion for you. This particular onion does have a core, which, in the case at hand, is the inverse of core, to wit—my exterior rotundity. In the course of my tale,

I shall arrive at the reason why you see before you a chap of sizable girth rather than a beanpole, in which slender state I first met your uncle some years ago. I think, Leo, you were shocked the other day when I re-introduced myself."

"Well, I recall a man who was *Tutt'occhi* — all eyes."

Worthington gave a quick, closed-mouthed triple *humph*, a slightly self-entertained laugh that made him quake. "All right." He closed his eyes and took a deep breath. "Let us say that when a person pulls the starter rope of an outboard motor he sets into motion those parts of the engine that cause it to run. When Uncle Leo here executed that innocent prank of his, involving the book of Leonardo Tron — this in conjunction with a pun on your Tron address — he likewise set into motion a series of events. How did this happen? Well..." He ran a hand across his thin, tightly combed-back silver hair. "I confess a share of responsibility in this matter. Until a few days ago, I ran a small year-old company called Kammerer Statistical. I took the name from Paul Kammerer, a scientist who during his short lifetime — he killed himself — was absorbed in the study of coincidence. I could have used the name *Jung*, as in *Carl Jung*, but Kammerer is less well known; his consideration of coincidences was more scientific, not 'acausal' or 'out of space and time,' as it was with Jung. I admit, however, that I am not one to choose among their merits. Both have fascinated me for years. Be that as it may, my organization, through the use of proprietary software, a most powerful suite of applications, tracked the coincidental repetitions of certain words and names as they appeared in hundreds of newspapers and other publications. I had one pet project — the name *Tron*. This was due solely to my interest in the mysterious books of Leonardo Tron, which I had heard about from a dying bibliophile years before. Despite his half-conscious and understandably slobbering disposition—rest in peace—I heeded his words and resolved to investigate. Nine months later, with a couple of clues in hand, I tracked down Tron's second book—only the second book, mind you; it led to a British official residing in the labyrinthine, cedar-scented medina of Fèz. In a cascade of scholarly falsehoods"—here Worthington gave his triple humph-laugh—"I persuaded his milquetoast male secretary to let me copy it. He granted my request, provided I copy it only by hand. But my transcription was cut short after only a few select pages; for a scandal arising from an appalling vice of the official, which abomination I shall not relate, caused him and his assistant to flee for their lives. They snatched up their basic possessions and left their house to be pillaged and partly burned. I should have kicked myself for not ransacking it along with the locals—even though emotions in the neighborhood were so enflamed that I'm sure my own life should have been endangered.

"I'll ignore my intermediate peregrinations and simply add that it was about a year after my trip to North Africa that I had a chance discussion—I should say *coincidental* discussion—in Rome's Fiumicino Airport with one of Leo's employees, who said he believed he knew where to find the first volume of Tron's work. To his credit he didn't tell me right away who possessed it but took my number and called me back after consulting with its owner. I was overcome with joy. Your uncle was extremely generous in allowing me make a full photographic copy of the work. I now possessed the complete text of Volume

One, which was a thought-provoking sixteenth-century discourse on what I came to realize reflected experiments in quantum physics. This branch of physics would not arise, of course, until several hundred years after Tron; and it would point to issues well beyond those of Newtonian physics, which blossomed a century after Tron's curious opus."

Worthington rested his cigar and took a sip of cream. His precise diction and the virtuosity of his impromptu sentence structure beguiled Rich and even made him envious. He also felt a touch of gratitude and even warmth toward him, as his tale-telling provided a much-needed, nerve-calming effect.

"More wanderings—through the brightest boulevards and the blackest alleys—brought me at length to" (another triple *humph*) "Istanbul. It was to there, among the architectural lineage of our present city, that I traced the journey of Volume Two out of that whitewashed, sweltering summer in Fèz. In short, I stole it from a spoiled and unsuspecting Turkish playboy, a revolting braggart, who used his books—which included rare medieval codices—as furniture. Blah! It was also there that I learned I was not the only person on the trail of Leonardo Tron's legendary tomes."

Rich interrupted. "So you do have, possess, volume two?"

"Yes—and well concealed, young man, I assure you. I haven't mentioned it to a soul until today—or yesterday. Having had the photographic copy of the first volume, I became the only person in centuries to have read the full text. As you and your girlfriend know only too well, others should like to have this privilege. Therefore, at this point I shall relate to you how these others showed their faces and, more important, what shadowy figure is behind their desperate and murderous quest."

Rich hunched forward, licked his lips, and wished he had some popcorn.

"As I stated, my company was engaged in the search for meaningful coincidences, my special interest in the surname *Tron* a personal project. This was initially to see whether any power adhered to the name, any cluster of coincidences which might call attention to activity in the world related to the books." He leaned forward and stared fixedly at Rich. "Soon my pursuit took on a new and important significance. My company was absorbed by a larger institution, whose name I cannot reveal, though it is known to your uncle. It is in the interest of this institution to penetrate the inmost circle of a certain individual who should like to add the works of Tron to his menagerie of manipulative engines. Whether the books have true power was always an open question with us; however, since we were in pursuit of physical objects, we hoped they might in some way leave a trail to the individual of whom I have just spoken. On the quantum level — a consideration we most certainly allowed — any activity associated with the name *Tron* might synchronistically provide one or more stepping stones to this person's forbidden lair."

Rich interrupted: "We're not talking about this Goodman Friendly, are we, the weird guy who kidnapped Simonetta?"

Leo shook his head and Worthington answered "No!" behind a cloud of smoke. "Friendly is a leftover hippy from Topanga Canyon, California, a demented one; a self-fancied prophet; was almost certainly involved in a pair of ritualistic killings out there. More recently he brainwashed young housewives with his corrupt interpretation of Tintoretto's paintings, pretending to be a reborn character in them or some such poppycock, finding the women's 'inner Jesus.' This he did for money and who knows what else—coitus, I'd venture. Perchance he came up with thought-exercises that obliquely echo the Tron theories."

"Yes, yes," Rich hissed thoughtfully, "it comes back to me. This is something I read about, I think."

"At present Friendly is connected with this other person, whom he has never met, and hopes to rise within his organization via possession of the books, which this secret individual ardently wishes to obtain."

Leo sat up straight. "It's the same with the others—the 'Rat Man,' as you call him, and the dead man in the crypt..."

"And what about that woman? Emma Mead, she called herself."

"That Tasmanian devil!"

"Ah! I was right."

"Small potatoes, my boy—*rotten* potatoes, rather. A maverick in my organization, a creature without conscience who snooped into private affairs. The less said of her, the better. All right, we've gotten ahead of ourselves. I should add that this Friendly-character stole a copy of my notes, the poor smattering of Book-Two notes I made during my ill-fated sojourn to Fèz. From what you told me earlier about the sweet and simple girl you met, I surmise that he misread certain passages and tried to force cockeyed mind-exercises on her, this beside his own leftover 'Topanga' material and other tommyrot of a similar nature.

"Where was I now? Yes, this is crucial. Several days ago my computers picked up unmistakable 'Tron activity.' Of course, this was the *Transfigured Night* article in *Il Gazzettino*, which you no doubt recall: three people, including you, seeing strange things all in one evening, all near a Tron location. Your own experience, of course, turned out to be a skit; the other two, if you want my opinion, were not in their right minds that night, for one reason or another. No matter, the coincidences were there and detected. The upshot would be understood: this was a signal—a sign of 'quantum coincidence,' which the presence of the books supposedly engendered—a signal that the remaining book was likely in Venice. What I did not know until the following day is that my computers recently had been, as they say, *hacked*, wantonly penetrated by that 'certain individual' I mentioned. In consequence, this fresh news about the Tron activity spread to one or two of his aspiring agents, who, scavengers that they are, or were, had nothing against committing murder for the privilege of delivering the coveted tomes. For the record, knowledge of your uncle's caprice, and of his plan to involve you and your girlfriend, occurred prior to the *Gazzettino* article. An operation was underway days earlier; for this 'certain individual,' or his close associates, snatched a year's worth of my electronic correspondence in the hacking, which led to the compromising of Leo's communications as well. I was foolish enough to send him a message about the book, which was still in his library. This was eleven months ago. Goodness! Can you imagine the red alert that caused!" He pulled a long white handkerchief from his interior pocket and passed it across his brow.

"Forgive me, Mr. Worthington, or Major, Mr. Major—"

"You may call me Major, both a first name and a rank. I grew into my name, you might say" (triple *humph).* Please note the *ton* in *Worthington,*" he added with mock solemnity.

Rich chortled politely. "Okay, there's a lot to digest."

"Let's don't talk digestion please." He held his stomach.

"I, uh... I'd like to know who murdered who—whom. I mean, those people who were looking for the book, were they all working for this mystery person you're referring to?"

"Yes, so how could they murder one another, you wonder?"

"That's right. I figure 'Rat Man'—or whatever his name is—killed the Asian guy, the guy we found in the crypt."

"He was Russian, actually—Vasily Kozlov, Siberian. 'Rat Man' is Bernhard Amsel, contrary to what his passport tells us."

"And I have a feeling this Friendly-crackpot did away with—what did you call him?—Amsel, 'Rat Man.' So, I mean..."

Worthington gave another triple *humph,* louder and with two or three jolly-sounding gulps. "Survival of the fittest, my boy, survival of the fittest. Such is the route to the top."

"So...this guy, head of the...secret order, mystery man..."

"All right now." Worthington sipped his cream. "How shall I proceed? Do you know that nowadays you can easily assemble your own radio station on the Internet? Further, do you know that you can have a whole television broadcasting system on a laptop computer—and for less than a thousand dollars?"

Rich shrugged with uncertain agreement.

"People today can do a lot with a little" — he raised a finger — "for good or for evil. Dare I part with Socrates and say that there are those who *knowingly* do evil, even for its own sake? Have you ever seen one of those amazing-hero movies — you know which ones — Supermen, Batmen, things of that variety?"

"When I was a kid, yes, some."

"Well, most people, you'll agree, identify more with the hero than with the villain."

Rich hummed affirmatively.

"Indeed. However, a small number do sympathize with the villain; and even if one could attribute this to a passing adolescent phase, and often correctly, I must tell you — and you must know this — that there are those who become overwhelmingly consumed with inspiration for the bad guy — and such a one is..."

Worthington leaned forward and scowled.

"Devlin Raptor."

Rich's brow shot up. "I heard Rat Man say that name. Devlin Raptor. Gosh, he *sounds* like an evil villain."

"His real name is Cory Schlitz."

"Cory?"

"From Keokuk, Iowa."

Rich rubbed his face.

"He started out by taking over his parents' old cellar, which, I have heard, he embellished with a dark Jurassic theme and which he constructed to go three levels below the original surface. Few people know where it is, or what he looks like. His specialty is mass persuasion, psycho-manipulation on a grand scale, a field destined to grow, I assure you, beyond our present understanding. I say *specialty*, but *hobby* is a better word. You see, we know about the big evil villains of the world—we read about them in the news, and we hope that the leaders of our democracies—together with our CIAs, MI6s and Mossads—can discover ways of dealing with them. Twenty-three-year-old Devlin Raptor, on the other hand, is what you might call a *tiny evil villain.* Of these hobbyists there is, alarmingly, a growing number; and he may well be the most ambitious of the brood."

Rich shook his head as if to expel a fly.

"This aspect was news to me also," Leo said.

"Fortunately, there are a growing number of those who do what I do, both within my larger organization and outside it."

"So, I mean, how...how did he get...to where he is, this Raptor guy? Three-story underground lair? Does he...have money?"

"He won the Powerball lottery, a lucrative U.S. game!"

"Madonnamì." Rich sighed, shaking off the fly again. He smoothed his bandage. "I have to get up and walk around."

"Take a breather, as they say. Stretch a bit. I'll go on."

Rich stood up and pressed his back to the wall; he exhaled loudly as he watched Leo gently smirk and nod his head.

Worthington continued: "It was Raptor and a clever friend who invented the ass-sparklers."

Rich cocked his head. His eyes moved to Leo and then to Worthington, who suppressed a laugh.

"Bum-beads, I like to call them."

Leo, studying the floor, chuckled audibly. Rich opened his mouth as if to speak but again did a comic freeze. Worthington gave his triple *humph* and proceeded: "I enjoy your reaction. You see, this tiny evil villain had a tiny evil project—in fact two projects, the second being the execution of the first. Small luminous beads—precisely arranged patterns of them—which when moved in a certain way subliminally flash a message, each bead a programmable word, each pattern a sentence. A subliminal grammar! Ingenious! The only problem was that the specialized motion needed to generate a message is too conspicuous for ordinary public use. Indeed, it turned out that the ideal movement is found only in the shimmying of the human ass!"

Rich's face crumpled; eyes closed, he heard Worthington's humph-laugh again and then bent over and let out a series of rippling, loud-mouthed guffaws that would not subside. He clasped his chair-back and slid down to a crouching position. Worthington and Leo contracted the infection and the fat man emitted loud ha-gulps, flab rippling in its elegant seat. Rich laughed out the expression *"hu-u-u-man ass!"*

"Il culo umano," Leo translated.

"Come, on, Leo!" Rich cried through his hilarity, still hugging the chair. "You're...you're fooling with me. This...this is a joke! It can't be real! This is...one of your...one of your damn pranks! The whole damn thing is one of your giant pranks!"

"No, Rich, I swear to you. It's real. It's true."

"Credo quia absurdum," Worthington noted. "Evermore, I'm afraid, in the fullness of time, more and more we'll find ourselves uttering that expression."

"Okay, okay..." Rich caught his breath. "I believe you." I think I witnessed the shimmy myself, as a matter of" — He stood up, recovering. "Oh... I needed that. Thanks. It was all pent up."

"We all needed it," Worthington affirmed.

Wiping his eyes, Rich sat back down. "Un-un-un-believable. Simply unbelievable."

"You know, of course, the pretty lagoon island of Burano; it's a tiny place noted for its lace-making, colorful house-fronts, and picturesque hanging laundry. It's a cupcake of an island about half an hour northwest of here by vaporetto."

Rich, catching his breath, slipped his glasses back on. "Yes, I've been there."

"Goodman Friendly happens to be fascinated with things Venetian—especially the carnival; he loves dress-up, and not only for perverse diversion; he has passports for each of his disguises. Well, through channels available to him—channels he earned—he got word to Devlin Raptor about the tiny island and what an excellent place it would be to test out the Bum-Beads. Indeed, space is limited there—in ten minutes you can walk from one end to the other—and the population is small. Now this island is perfect for—"

A female voice. *"Ciao, tutti!"* Everyone looked. Simonetta, wrapped in a paisley blanket and wearing a black and yellow ski cap with matching booties, appeared from around a bend.

"Ah, I told you she'd be all right," boasted Worthington.

Rich and Leo stood up and greeted her with hugs and expressions of triumph and affection. *"Mi sento assolutamente bene,"* she reassured them, "I feel toe-tally ok-ay," she added in her cute mechanical English. "But, Reech"—she noted his bandage—*"Cosa ti è successo?"* (What happened to you?)

"I'll tell you later. It's okay. This is Major Worthington. The man Uncle Leo told us about."

Simonetta greeted him with quick once-over, her cordial face sparring with a look of surprise. She sat down and stretched out on the remaining empty chair. "I'm not sure what happened," she continued in Italian. "I know I was a fool for following that guy and photographing him. I should have run the other way."

"You said it," Leo admonished. "And you messed up a major sting we had worked out. Then Rich tried to rescue you."

She purred with endearment, questioningly.

"Dumb thing," Rich whined. "I'll tell you later."

She put her fingers to her temples. "What was I was saying? 'Down with clotheslines, up with laundromats?' My mouth was not my own. It was weird!"

"You've come at the right moment, my dear. I was about to explain this aspect—I think that's what you referred to, if my comprehension of spoken Italian serves me—though you won't grasp everything. I was speaking about the tiny, colorful island of Burano, famed among other things for its picturesque hanging laundry, an aspect of the place that photographers love so well. The project I started to mention was never initiated—the Tron affair got in the way—but all during the carnival period, Goodman Friendly—the freakish bloke you two called the Lion Man—was supposed to be stationed on the island, in a strategic location frequented by locals, in which spot, sporting his clownish mane, he was to jiggle his flickering fundament, delivering subliminally the same message he abused you with, my dear, which in your case he did, I'm sure, out of pure wantonness and perhaps frustration at not finding Book Two. Speaking of the second book, we believed, of course, that he had planned to leave soon—even today—for Milan to find that boy who vomited on the Tron Bridge. He obviously wouldn't have found the book there, for I possess it."

Simonetta squinted. "I don't reel-ly fol-low," she whined, having difficulty with Worthington's long English sentences.

"Yes, what about Burano again?" Rich inquired.

"Well, you understand what a perfect test-site the petite island is. How easy to track little by little the disappearance of hanging laundry — and the rise of laundromats and their dryers — as the locals became infused with the controlling message. It was only to be an exercise to observe the efficacy of the system. Imagine its use in advertising or politics. I told you that Devlin Raptor's specialty was mass control. Just think of its usefulness in the swaying of opinions, sentiment-building within a whole nation."

"Do you suppose it would work, at that level?"

"It wears off fast, as we see. However, beware the horizon, you two! Danger lurks in development! In future, it will be difficult to distinguish between pranks, crimes, and acts of war. The individual will fail to see the prankish nature of his own doings — and beliefs. Worse, imagine the day when people will be able to change themselves — deface themselves — into dogs or trees or puddles, benign or vicious. Then lion men or rat men will truly walk the earth! I am not sure which has more potential for terror, people, groups of people, or governments. I'm being rhetorical, of course. The answer is — all three. How vulnerable the sifted nectar of civilization!" (Single cheerless *humph.*)

Rich removed his glasses and rubbed his eyes.

"Things develop rapidly," Leo sighed in a wistful tone that Rich thought reflected his having been away from his field for a while. Rich graciously put in, "But you certainly had no problem tackling these...new things, Uncle Leo."

"Well, I'm lucky. My connections are still loyal."

Worthington slapped his chunky thighs. "And now," he announced as if to provide a cymbal crash before the tonic resolution, "the final mystery — why I became so fat! I know that your uncle once described me to you as an extremely skinny chap; and so I was — a mere slither; if I turned sideways I practically vanished" (triple *humph)*. "Well, I'll show you to what I owe my present girth and then connect my fabulous flab to the whole."

Beside his chair rested a stout black briefcase that resembled a doctor's bag. He slid it around and positioned it between his highly polished wingtip shoes. He opened its wide mouth and, with a huff, reached down inside it with both hands. "Here it is," he said with hushed gravity; "we found it in Friendly's slovenly flat. Many thanks to Leo for its donation."

It was a surprisingly small volume, only slightly larger than the palm it rested on. Rich recognized the dull pearly cover as vellum, a material used for centuries in the production of books. For a second he thought it glowed. The cover was plain, with dark smudges, scuffs, and rust-colored foxing at the edges. Worthington opened the book. The title, "I RADICI VIVENTI DELLA POSSIBILITÀ" (THE LIVING ROOTS OF POSSIBILITY), in large capitals, was centered on two lines at the top followed by the smaller, lower caste "Discorso Pratico" (Practical Discorse), beneath which *"Diviso in Due Libri"* (Divided into Two Books) appeared in italics, followed by "PRIMO" and *"Opera Scritta Da"* (work written by) and the author's name in smaller capitals. At the bottom was the date, "MDXLIV." The frontispiece was blank and no publisher's mark or decorative elements were present.

"The small octavo format, the griffo-style italics of the main text, much is reminiscent, in spotty way, of Manuzio's Aldine Press. Of course, it cannot be; for one thing, the subject matter is not in keeping with that press. Rather, I believe it a Florentine imitation of the style. It's in pure *lingua Toscana*. I should guess it was a private, even secret printing. Not the kind of thing you should want to have around in the Cinquecento. Pity, because Venice was so open to ideas in the century before, with the blossoming of the presses." He held up the book and sighed. "Too bad it's mostly bullshit!" He bent over and lowered it into his bag.

Rich widened his eyes, aware of his own comic reaction.

"Pardon my language, young lady." He snapped his bag shut. "I admit that this book, the first volume, is thought-provoking. Hauntingly, there may even be some truth in it. The second book, well, with all the rot about *creating* coincidences, is nothing more than a pile of *caca* so great you cannot see the top of it!"

"You mean much ado about—"

"*Niente*, yes, but it's a nice collector's item. And I do believe everything in the universe is, in a sense, unmanifest without the 'magic lamp' of consciousness."

Rich relaxed into a pensive pose.

"My becoming fat, however—now *that* is what highlights the true importance of the work. You see, my erstwhile svelte appearance became known to Raptor's minions. They had photographs of me; they knew me. I went into hiding, in presumed retirement, withdrawal, making by way of the Internet and other avenues certain, well, connections I needed to have. In brief, I built a socially undesirable reputation, at the same time feasting on the world's richest cuisines to obliterate my known appearance. How sick am I of Fettuccine Alfredo!" He made a deranged face and clasped his belly. "But, you see" — he reached for his glass of cream — "it's an addiction that's hard to relinquish." He took a satisfying sip. "I must impress upon you that Friendly, and the others, needed to possess the volumes to reach the rewarding inner circle of Raptor's society — in short, to meet him in person. Without bearing coveted gifts, approach would be impossible. They needed to prove themselves. The books were the ticket. Now *I* have the books. *I* hold the ticket." He leaned over and rapped the leg of the settee with his knuckles. "Knock on wood."

Rich sighed. "The world gets stranger by the minute. So what will you do with his 'tiny evil villain' when you get to him?"

Worthington lowered his brow, leaned forward. "Give him a not-so-tiny spanking, of course!" He let out a snarling triple *humph*.

Rich was too dazed to inquire further.

***

Passengers gazing out of vaporetto 4.1 on the breezy route from the cemetery island of San Michele to the Fondamenta Nuove were shocked into revulsion. Lodged between the raw conjoined stumps of a *bricola* — a bound triad of logs marking a navigational route — was a swollen, doe-pale face with squashed mouth. One eye and the flesh beneath it was lumped out like an exposed bulb, the eyelid opening and closing flirtatiously in the wind; it seemed almost to serve a useful purpose as a light does on a buoy. Shopkeepers on the *fondamenta* connected the corpse with a handsome dark-haired "English woman" who, in passing, had fiercely wielded a small umbrella and blathered about laundry.

Chapter Five

Rich dropped the newspaper to his knees.

Omigod, she's dead. I wiped that woman's nose a few days ago and now she's dead. How weird is that!

He looked at his wastepaper basket and knew that her tissue-wrapped discharge lived there still.

The newspapers brimmed with conjecture about "special operations" or "exercises" that had taken place in Venice. The lead sentence of every item asked whether it was the GIS *(Gruppo di Intervento Speciale)* or the NOCS *(Nucleo Operativo Centrale di Sicurezza)* or another special unit that had, for an unknown reason, descended on a vacant Santa Croce palazzo. "Who were those masked men who vanished as quickly as they came?"

Only one paper hinted at a possible connection between the SWAT assault and the "sudden appearance of costumed lecturers" around the city; but this observation was a carnival quip by a reporter who may have wanted to reserve credit for his deduction without committing to a serious statement. Every paper, however, asked whether a link existed between the three recent deaths and the SWAT operation, though the police proved murder in only one case.

Rich lifted himself off the sofa, yawned, and ran his fingers through his hair. He stared at the open bedroom door and remembered the man he saw on the roof—Leo's fellow prankster—a week before. He wandered into the bedroom and gazed out at the sun-starved morning. So much had happened in seven days. He hated losing touch with his usual life, his familiar routine. He wondered what he would be doing right now, what he would be thinking. How was life different? For one thing, Simonetta more than ever had entered his daily movements. She had not been around much before and now she was with him every single day.

Leo pulled that one off all right.

For another, their whole adventure stained a part of his spirit like an inky dye. He knew, however, that it was a question of time: someday it would be fun to remember it.

She knows how to enjoy the regular present.

Simonetta was out this morning buying a new cell phone, as her old one was at the bottom of a canal. She said she would call.

He returned to the sofa and stretched out on it, staring at the beamed ceiling. He wondered how long he himself would be around. Venice was perhaps the most expensive city in Europe.

I've probably got thirty days left.

Last evening he recapped for Simonetta the complete discourse of Major Worthington. He also told her his days in Venice were numbered. She swallowed hard and adjusted her face to hide what he thought was a deeper sadness than what she showed. "I know a whole lot of people," she said half to herself later on, "but have few, hardly any, real friends." Rich thought the comment born of thin air, as they had been off the subject of his leaving and were talking about the gondoletta. He informed her that he, too, had very few friends. He was sorry he said it, since he uttered it with an insouciant chuckle. He thought it sounded as if he wanted to outdo her loneliness.

Privately he felt the need to return to his creative world without a social tie he thought might highjack his inspiration. He sensed this world was a love-life in itself. Back home, at about eight, he continued work on his new poem and finished it. Now he slid it off the coffee table and read it again:

Carved like cuckoo clocks these Bavarian chambers and with banners from the rafters sills of steins emblems long dark tables a kind of heraldic cavern to be lived in. Against the warmth of hearth and glow of wine snow showers beyond the leaded windows and the band a whispered memory. We all of us told tales of kindred elsewheres in the mountains: the mystery village I came upon—not on any map—slope-side chalet nuzzled in a snowy grove but still within the whole of spattered dwellings: tall windows between day and night with hot black tea and the angled reveries of spangled seasons. In the snug little garret of book-eyes drowsy under warm and rustic tufts the lamplight's soft and dreamy. Within the lodge a mystery in the night: the proprietor saw a phosphorescent something—a jagged fidgety figure lighting down a rise. "I tell you mister 'olmes it wernt no human bean." On an opposite slope in another chalet a stately blonde stirs a bowl of lilies — gently...gently: Sir George's eyes to sleep... sleep...sleep... I awaken slightly: white marble theater long ago in a world of simple days—the fabulous Venetian future unthought-of in invisible quiet. No—I meant Sir George the man not Saint James the theater. Here I dip again: Paris: Hotel Le Bristol. No. Well...Goodbye. Perhaps I shall return.

It was not a mansion poem, not one of those favorites filled with involuntary flecks of times past that rush into the present and hint of the Everlasting. Rather, it was purely a comfort poem, which, beyond the clearly rendered Bavarian lodge, brought forth (by way of a fleck or two) cozy old Sherlock Holmes movies and a long-gone picture palace he knew as a child, which in the poem flecked off of itself an elegant Paris hotel he once stayed at. After that point, he knew he lost the lodge-flecks and quit.

Later last night, in bed, he watched the 1940 film *Our Town*, a movie based on Thornton Wilder's play. He dozed off right after the cemetery scene, his favorite part of the movie, with Aaron Copland's stunningly perfect score lulling him to sleep.

He got up from the sofa and sighed. "I shall but love thee better after death," he said aloud, quoting Elizabeth Barrett Browning, whose famous line epitomized the Romantic Movement.

That's the trick, of course,

He would retreat a year or two and she would enter the Realm, distant days together charged with flecks of —

"Afar," he whispered.

What a beautiful word.

"Afar."

Then he would return for the glorious recapture, the "near-and-far."

If recapture is possible. And if...she'll have me.

His phone rang. He dug it out of his pocket. It was Simonetta.

"I made a new Tron discovery!" she announced.

"What again? You're still at it? How's the new phone?"

"I got the same kind. I'll show you what I found when we get together. Let's meet at that nice restaurant off the Calle del Carbone. We can sit in their covered patio with all the plants. I feel like greenery. Leave right now, okay?"

Seconds after she said *greenery* and hung up, welcome sun cheered the windows and the front room of the apartment. The new light and the thought of green plants made him spring from the sofa and whistle a melody from Respighi's *Pini di Roma.*

Look, I'm whistling.

Simonetta's keen disposition topped off the happy concurrence and all at once his Tron memories lost their caustic gloom.

There's still lightness in me. Tron will go away.

Soon he was outside in the spring-like weather wearing only a light jacket. In a couple of minutes, after making a left, a right and another left, he passed under the short Sotopòrtego de le Muneghe. He made another right and was about to cross the Ponte del Teatro with its fancy metal railings, when he heard a woman call out, *"Scusi, signore!"* He turned and saw a tall, smiling middle-aged woman with bobbed copper hair. She wore a tan suede jacket, a black skirt and a close-fitting string of plump faux pearls. Apparently she had just left the supermarket, whose doors and bank of tall windows faced the foot of the bridge.

"*Signora?*" he gently questioned.

"I'm sorry to disturb you, but I think I know you."

"Really?"

"Well, I don't actually know you, but weren't you at Leo's party last week on the last night of *Carnevale?*"

"Yes, I was, in fact. I was there." Then a mild electrical current ran through him.

Omigod, it's Simonetta's mother I'll bet.

"I saw you. You were with my daughter, Simonetta."

He infused himself with cordiality. "Oh, what a pleasure! So glad to meet you!" They shook hands.

I guess I am. Yes, I really am. It's okay. It's good.

"I'm Marisa Leoni-Ballarin. I said to my husband, 'Who's that nice young man?' You're Reech, right? And your surname?"

"Travella." He pressed his chin to secure his two band-aids.

"Listen," she continued, and she smacked him on the arm in the same friendly way his mother does when reinforcing a point. "Simonetta told me you love old movies. I do too! For a long time I've been wanting to start a kind of movie night at our house. Once a week, say, or every two weeks. Maybe you can help me with it—you know, selecting titles and everything."

"Oh sure, sure." He thought of mentioning his looming departure from Venice but held off as not to deflate her appealing suggestion. "That's a great idea." He meant it.

They crossed the bridge and continued chatting, mostly about Clark Gable and Myrna Loy. He told her the two actors had made seven or eight movies together, not as many as the team of Powell and Loy, which, if he remembered correctly, was fourteen. "I love William Powell!" she exclaimed. *"Simpaticissimo!"*

They parted outside the Campiello della Chiesa, next to the bank, and she kissed him on both cheeks and patted his shoulders. "I'll call Simonetta and we'll all get together."

What a nice lady. Very appealing mannerisms. I did okay.

Five minutes later he entered the see-through patio-tent of the restaurant, moving aside large leaves to get to Simonetta, whose back was to him. "So what's this new Tron stuff you found?" he asked outright instead of saying *ciao.*

"Tesorino!" she exclaimed.

"Guess who I met a minute ago? Your *mamma!"* He sat down and filled her in on the movie-night idea, rocking his head with reserved uncertainty. Simonetta likewise fidgeted; and he perceived that she, too, tried to deflect allusion to his looming departure. "I really like the idea," he proclaimed, calculating a touch of regret in his eyes.

"Yes, *bell'idea,"* she added. I more or less knew about it. Well now..." She took a sheet of paper from her small case and slapped her palms over it. "We didn't talk much about it yesterday, but" — she furrowed her brow and patted the table — "I want to know... Do you think there was anything, you know, really, I mean *genuinely* mystical about all that happened?"

Rich leaned back and took a deep breath. "I've been tossing the question around too." Well, I mean, a lot of things that look like coincidences — I mean mystical coincidences—aren't or weren't. I was thinking... I mean, look at Leo's name—Leo Leoni. It has nothing to do with Ornella believing she saw a lion on the arch. And the author's name—Leonardo. And the guy we called Lion Man, because of his hair—that was nothing more than accidental, no? And—what's his name?—the boy—Tonio; he saw a flaming baby, which has nothing to do with anything."

"The Tron-Piavola Bridge, though. I told you *Piavola* means *doll* in Venetian. But maybe he knew that."

"Unconsciously maybe. Nevertheless, there's no connection. *Doll* has nothing to do with anything else."

"Right."

"I mean, the name *Tron* is all over the place. The family was entrenched in Venetian history. The first operas in Venice were held in a Tron theater. There's a Campiello Tron and Fondamenta Tron over in Dorsoduro, a Rio Tron. The Church of San Stae, where we were all around the other day, may have been started by the Tron family; there's the Palazzetto Tron-Memmo; There's Niccolò Tron's magnificent tomb in the Frari, which is famous. The Tron shield is even on a wall in some calle, I forget which, so..."

"But I met the kid, gave him a lift the night of the party. He was on the Tron bridge. I met him."

"Okay, that's a pretty good one. But who knows how many delusional kids were out that night, drinking, whatever..."

"That's irrelevant, tesorino."

"I'll bet even the arch by Ornella's was part of the Tron estate. The palazzo is nearby. Anyway, the dominoes started falling with Worthington's computers being hacked, right? God, all that stuff!

'Tiny evil villain.' 'Ass-Twinklers.' I think his tale is as weird as anything else we've seen or heard, no?"

"What about you and the plum-pudding guy, the old man you said looked like Leo's friend on your roof?"

He hummed in agreement. "And me thinking of plum pudding and seeing the Carl Jung book. I admit that's a tough one. Of course, I saw the old man awhile ago. Could it have been a distorted memory?"

She puckered her face. "You're running away from it again, you! You know that the guy was behind the Palazzo Tron."

"Yes, well... Remember what Worthington said later? About coincidence being a natural state of the world and the mind? There are—what did he say?— different *bandwidths* or something we're not aware of and we might fall into one of these zones and start seeing coincidences and so forth... I don't know."

"I don't know either." She exhaled resignedly and then opened her eyes widely. "However!" she growled, turning the word into an accusation. She looked at her sheet of paper.

He shook his head and grunted back a laugh.

"Have you examined the names of those people who saw a strange thing that first night, including your own name? Okay, your initials—*R.T.* Ornella's is *O.R.* Ornella Riusi, right?"

Already Rich had lowered his head close to the tabletop, nodding with incipient laughter.

"Tonio Occhini, the drugged-up kid who saw the flaming baby or whatever the hell it was—his initials are *T.O.* His real name is Antonio, but he called himself *Tonio.* Look!" She slapped the paper down in from of him. Written on the page was, *TRO, TRO.*

189

"Simonetta, you are a crazy girl. So who's *N.N.*?? There's got to be a Nino Nardi or a...Nanette Newfoundland or a person with those initials involved somewhere we don't know about."

"We'll never know!" she squealed, making her scrunchy "popcorn" face. She shot a single-note, ear-splitting laugh.

"You are a crazy little eel. But wait a minute! You see, it's all a regular coincidence. In Latin, the abbreviation *N.N.* means *nomen nescio* or *name unknown* — literally, *I do not know the name*. So, you see, we really don't know the name, assuming there is a name to know, which there probably isn't. Are we going to order or what? Let's look at the menu — *mannaggia*."

She made a loony, siren-like sound. "I guess it's always like that, with this mystical stuff. You never know. I'm having the reginette al pesto Genovese. Want to split a caprese?"

"Genovese, caprese... Italian is full of rhymes like the world is full of coincidences. *Uff, basta!* Drop the subject. Yes, all right, the caprese and the...*pasta*. I'm tired of thinking. No, I'll have the bigoli in salsa. It doesn't rhyme with *caprese*."

"I have another thing for you to think about, but I'll save it for dessert."

"*Mamma mia*," he groaned. "Prosecco for me, a full bottle!"

"*Papà!*" she exclaimed, looking past him.

No, this can't be.

She stood up and he looked over his shoulder. A slim, handsome man in a blue and green madras shirt and cream-colored jacket approached from the other side of the patio.

Stand up...stand up. Look delighted.

She threw her arms around her father, kissing him. *Babbino caro,* this is my friend Reech Travella.

"Ah, Reech!" he declared with warm satisfaction, holding out his hand. "The famous Reech! *Che piacere!* Happy to know you at last."

They shook hands and Rich drew from his stock of cordial attitudes, in this case tightening his lips and rocking his head. "Oh, it's a pleasure to meet you too."

It is... I guess it really is. It's okay. I'm okay.

"Papà, sit down, have something. Where's our waiter?"

"No no, just passing. I saw your little round coconut through the greenery." He affectionately cupped her head, messing her hair. "Say, Reech, I've been wanting to meet you. Simonetta told me about the photos you take—reflections in the canals, the textures of walls and so forth."

"Oh yes, I've got hundreds of those."

Sit down. Now's the proper time.

"You know, I'm in the textile business. We have a home-decorating division—you know, a lot of tiles of various kinds, different materials. I was thinking about a line that draws from Venetian textures. I'd like to see your work to get some ideas."

"Oh, that would be great. That's a fine idea."

"Here comes the waiter. Okay, I'm going. Got a meeting at the bank over here. Reech, let's stay in touch! I heard you two had an adventure. I want to hear about it. Ciao-ciao!"

Simonetta did the ordering. "What's the matter, Reech?"

He scratched his temple and narrowed one eye. "I, uh, hate revisit our, uh, favorite subject again, but..."

"Subject? What subject?"

He snorted and looked down. "I mean..."

She reached under her chair for her thin zippered briefcase. "You mean coincidences? Let me show you this now. I can't wait for later." She took out a newspaper clipping and handed it to him. "It was in several papers this morning. It might interest you."

CERCASI BIBLIOTECARIO PRIVATO

Distinguished Venetian gentleman offers full-time, live-in position cataloging and maintaining large personal library. Generous compensation. Suite of rooms and gourmet meals provided. Scholarly background preferred.

Rich squinted at the ad and nodded, nodded, his tongue massaging the inside of one cheek.

"What do you say to that, Reech?"

Still nodding, he drew in his lips to squelch a smirk.

"You know, speaking of jobs, or not speaking of jobs" — she tittered — "I think I'm going to sell my little newspaper. Uncle Leo set me up in it, and I'm very grateful, but I'm not cut out for it. Maybe I can get his money back. Actually, you know, I think I would like take up his old profession, something along that line. You know, a kind of secret-secret service thing, where you arrange stuff, scenarios — but to help individual people. I would charge for it, of course. What do you think?"

Rich looked at the arriving waiter. "I think our prosecco is here." He met Simonetta's stare. At the *pop* of the cork he stood up, leaned toward her at the sound of the fizz. She lifted herself half way as he took her coconut head in his hands. They closed their eyes and fed deeply on each other's lips.

**

It became a largely wordless lunch. Everything had already been covered and now only a calm afterglow remained. They parted with a promise to meet again for dinner. An urge that resisted definition moved Rich to wander, and he made his way south across the San Marco district. He halted at the end of the Calle dei Fabbri, at the steps of the Ponte dei Dai, a bridge that leads under an arch and through an arcade of shops that opens brightly into Piazza San Marco. He pondered the word *dai*, an exclamation used to egg one on or "go for it!" Tradition holds that the name of the bridge derives from the encouraging cries of people behind the Bajamonte-Tiepolo conspirators, who in 1310 tried to subvert the government. In old texts, however, it was called *Ponte dei Dadi*, meaning *Bridge of Dice*, perhaps because gamers would use this spot for their competitions.

I guess nothing is certain. It's a roll of the dice.

He crossed the bridge, passed through the *sotopòrtego* of shops and emerged in sunny Piazza San Marco under a flight of pigeons. Save for tenacious confetti on the gray stone pavement, all evidence of the carnival was gone; and he sensed that the great basilica was its center-piece self again. People strolled, as did many pigeons; and the four-piece band outside the Caffè Florian played a tango for a dozen customers seated in the tope-and-chrome wicker-style chairs at the outdoor tables.

He strolled diagonally toward the campanile and then into the Piazzetta, alongside the Ducal Palace and a sea of outdoor tables belonging to other cafes. He made the decision not to walk between the two granite columns, the one with the winged lion on top and the other with Saint Theodore; it was bad luck to do so, as the Republic had executed and dangled traitors there. He wondered if nowadays we would call the pillars the *Columns of Sighs*; after all, a condemned man's last sight would be the currently adjacent Chanel N°5 poster with its sensual perfume-spraying model.

He rounded the bend, past more tables, and hiked into the avenue of souvenir kiosks that front the little park or *giardinetto*. There he turned toward the water, went over to the long balustrade and rested, leaning into a light, fresh breeze. It was one of his favorite spots; he looked to his right at the gleaming Dogana, the old Customs House, on the tapered tip of Dorsoduro, where the Grand Canal ends; beyond the customs he gazed toward a long, floating piece of the island of Giudecca and then left to the tidy isle of San Giorgio Maggiore with its tower echoing Saint Mark's in miniature. In the aquatic distance the thin spine of the Lido sealed the hazy blue horizon.

How was all this possible?

Even with all the histories he had read of Venice it was still hard to grasp visually how the descendants of terrified mainland people, who fled the barbarians in the wake of the Roman Empire, turned swampy puzzle-pieces of terrain, with salt galore but no crops or building materials at hand, into the wealthiest, most powerful empire in Europe, one that held dominion over the Adriatic and most of the Eastern Mediterranean.

I would love to see a time-lapse movie of it.

His reverie broke when his phone rang in his pocket.

"Mom!"

"Hi, Richaaard!" she sang in her effervescent manner. "Say, listen, I'm taking a trip. Guess what."

"What?"

I'm coming to Venice!"

"What!"

"Yeah, me, Aunt Betty and Sadie Matarazzo's sister Mildred. Next week. We're coming to see you. You know Mildred. She's a real card."

"That's great! How did this happen? When did you —?"

"Oh, I was just thinking. You know me, I'm always thinking."

They chatted more about the trip. Rich told her about Simonetta's mother and her love of classic movies. Before they hung up with the customary love and kisses, he suspected, correctly, how the idea of her voyage had come into being. His mother, bless her (and her voice), was not adept at concealing a charade.

Ah, the Leo clan.

"A long reach; they have a very long reach."

Like the Venetian Empire.

The word *reach* reminded him of Simonetta's pronunciation of his name. This made him think about his full name — Rich Travella. He recalled from way back that both Freud and Jung had noted a coincidental similarity between people's names and certain things about them. The name *Travella* contained the English word *travel*, and he acknowledged gratefully that he was in fact a rich traveler — and a very lucky one. Indeed, with a slight blush he considered how much better he had it than those early Venetians: buildings ready-made for him, trade routes and ports in place.

Except my poetry and writing. I'll have to figure that out. It might be okay. Yeah... I guess.

He scuffed back a step.

There's this weird week too — ready to be set down. I could bring my flecks into it somehow. It might work. What's a good title?

He thought of the line by surrealist poet Jean Cocteau about Venice being a city "where pigeons walk and lions fly."

Yeah, and where Rich gets hitched and can still procreate.

He looked up at the cloudless heavens —

Hey, stranger things have happened, right?

—and made a whisking sign of the cross.

ABOUT THE AUTHOR

Peter Lucia was born and raised on the New Jersey Shore, where he still resides. He has degrees from Columbia University in Italian Studies with a very high concentration in Philosophy (both of which come together in *One Week in Venice*). He taught Italian as a graduate student at Columbia and Italian and English at Berlitz School of Languages in Los Angeles and Beverly Hills. His serious hobbies (and sometime-professions) include classical guitar, which he has played and studied, off and on, since the mid-1960s, computer art, photography, travel to Italy, local history, and writing. He often contributes these skills and interests to the personal projects of friends and family. He has no dogs, no cats, no wife, and no kids.

Also by Peter Lucia

"The Murder at Asbury Park"